WE BUILT THIS CITY

Cat Patrick

 Nancy Paulsen Books

NANCY PAULSEN BOOKS
An imprint of Penguin Random House LLC, New York

First published in the United States of America by Nancy Paulsen Books,
an imprint of Penguin Random House LLC, 2024

Copyright © 2024 by Cat Patrick

Penguin supports copyright. Copyright fuels creativity, encourages diverse voices, promotes free speech, and creates a vibrant culture. Thank you for buying an authorized edition of this book and for complying with copyright laws by not reproducing, scanning, or distributing any part of it in any form without permission. You are supporting writers and allowing Penguin to continue to publish books for every reader.

Nancy Paulsen Books & colophon are trademarks of Penguin Random House LLC.
The Penguin colophon is a registered trademark of Penguin Books Limited.

Visit us online at PenguinRandomHouse.com.

Library of Congress Cataloging-in-Publication Data
Names: Patrick, Cat, author.
Title: We built this city / Cat Patrick.
Description: New York: Nancy Paulsen Books, 2024. |
Summary: As Stevie tours with her sign-language group during the summer of 1985, she writes to famous radio jockey Casey Kasem to reveal her feelings toward her crush live over the air.
Identifiers: LCCN 2023019097 (print) | LCCN 2023019098 (ebook) |
ISBN 9780593462164 (hardcover) | ISBN 9780593462171 (ebook)
Subjects: CYAC: Friendship—Fiction. | Interpersonal relations—Fiction. |
Sign language—Fiction. | Deaf—Fiction. | LCGFT: Novels.
Classification: LCC PZ7.P2746 We 2024 (print) |
LCC PZ7.P2746 (ebook) | DDC [Fic]—dc23
LC record available at https://lccn.loc.gov/2023019097
LC ebook record available at https://lccn.loc.gov/2023019098

Printed in the United States of America

ISBN 9780593462164

1st Printing
LSCH

Edited by Stacey Barney
Design by Cindy De la Cruz
Text set in Carre Noir Pro, Pump Pro

This book is a work of fiction. Any references to historical events, real people, or real places are used fictitiously. Other names, characters, places, and events are products of the author's imagination, and any resemblance to actual events or places or persons, living or dead, is entirely coincidental.

The publisher does not have any control over and does not assume any responsibility for author or third-party websites or their content.

For Brad

Keep your feet on the ground and keep reaching for the stars.

—Casey Kasem

1.

THE FIRST TIME I saw Joey, I fell out of a maple tree.

It was a summer Saturday morning, and my best friend, Wes, and I were waiting for Synchronicity rehearsal to start at an Episcopal church downtown. A few of the older kids in the cast weren't there yet, and the director—Wes's mom, Margo—was pacing around the community room, muttering about curfews, respect, and the ultimate threat, calling parents.

Wes and I fled so Margo wouldn't make us do chores like wiping down the star boxes or ironing costumes. The following week, everyone thirteen and up would leave for August tour, but Wes and I weren't old enough yet.

"Brandon's so lucky," I said, meaning my older brother. Our mom had labeled every piece of his clothing with his initials. I wanted my clothing labeled! "I can't wait until we can tour."

I laid my hand on my peeling sunburnt thigh and let a wandering ant climb aboard, then relocated it to a nearby leaf. Afraid of heights, I was saddled on the thickest, lowest branch, back against the rough trunk, bark poking me in the spine. Wes was two levels up, sneakered feet dangling high overhead.

"Totally," he said before popping his gum. "I want to go somewhere new. I've never been anywhere."

"Me neither. Except the time my family went to Iowa to visit my grandparents. A tire blew on the highway, and we almost died."

"How old were you?"

"Like three. We hadn't met yet. I don't even remember it; they just told me."

"Doesn't count, then."

"Duh."

Wes and I had known each other since we were five, when our moms were on a bowling team and threw us in the kid corral at the bowling alley together; anything before that didn't matter.

"It's good you didn't die, though," Wes said. "Hey, want to go to Time-Out later? I found a bunch of tokens under Shannon's bed."

"Sure, there's a lip-synch battle in the atrium. I heard my brother talking about it."

"Rad, so a lot of people will be there. Even . . ."

"Who?"

"Those girls might be there," he said carefully. I didn't respond at first. "Did you hear me?"

"Yeah, so what about the Jennifers?" I asked, ferrying another confused ant to safety. Jennifer T. had just moved in across the street at the beginning of the summer and was already best friends with Jennifer R., who we went to elementary school with.

"They like swimming, and you do, too."

"So? You sound like my mom." I rolled my eyes. My mom was always trying to get me to talk to people. She said I was shy, and that shy people got ignored in life, but I talked plenty to my family, Wes, and my castmates. "I don't need more friends. I'm fine with you."

"Okay," Wes said. He could probably tell I felt weird, because he changed the subject. "What's for dinner tonight?" He ate at our house more than at his own.

"Ham and pineapple," I said, mock gagging as a tan station wagon pulled into the parking lot, squeaking over the speed bump before it stopped. The car windows were down, so I could hear Casey Kasem introducing the next song on the *American Top 40 Countdown*. "The Eastridge car pool's here."

"Oh yeah?"

I smiled, knowing what Wes wanted to know. Leafy branches

were in his way of seeing whether his big-time crush was part of the car pool. I noted the kids as they climbed out of the car: brothers Shane and Trevor Buchanan, Cassandra Schwartz . . .

"Tuesday's with them," I said, giggling. Wes had been totally in love with Tuesday Thomas since forever. "Tuesday and Wes, sitting in a tr—"

"Knock it off."

"K-I-S-S-I-N-G."

"For reals, knock it off."

I opened my mouth to continue to do the opposite of knocking it off—but then someone I'd never seen before got out of the station wagon, and it felt like my whole world screeched to a halt. I didn't even care that there was, like, a whole colony of ants on my legs.

"Who is *that*?" I asked quietly.

The first thing I thought was that the boy looked like a model in a shampoo commercial. His dark hair shined as if he'd combed it three-and-a-half seconds ago, and it was parted down the middle, longer in the back, feathered to perfection. He was dressed in the kind of outfit that every boy I knew wore every other day—a white ringer tee with dark blue sleeves, tan dolphin-hem shorts with white piping, and tall sports socks with white high-tops—but the mystery guy somehow wore his clothes *better*.

"Who's who?" Wes asked.

"You're an owl," I murmured, watching the stranger. I wondered if he had soft skin; I'd never wondered about a person's skin before.

"No, because owls have great vision, and I can't see a thing."

"You shouldn't climb up so high."

It was a miracle I was able to carry on a conversation with Wes, I was so distracted. While the boy and Shane joked around, the station wagon idled, the music still playing, a soundtrack to the moment.

I watched as Shane introduced the boy to another cast member—the boy extended his hand confidently. He was cute and polite! Shane laughed at something the boy said; he was funny, too! I giggled like I'd heard the joke, heart beating fast, jittery all of a sudden. And the music didn't do anything to chill my urgent and immediate crush feelings because no matter when, no matter what song, music *totally* made everything more emotional.

The new kid ran his hands through his shampoo-commercial hair before saying something, making everyone around him bust up. I laughed like I was part of the conversation.

"What's so funny?"

"I don't know. He knows Shane."

"Who knows Shane?"

"I don't know! It's a new kid!"

The cutest new kid I've ever seen in my life.

The new kid who's going inside the community room right now.

"Let's go in," I said quickly, wanting to know the new kid's name . . . and everything about him! Where had he come from? What grade was he going into? Where did he live? (Probably Eastridge.) How did he know Shane? How did he know about Synchronicity? What was he like? Was he *actually* a shampoo-commercial model?

"But all of the high schoolers aren't even here yet," Wes groaned. "My mom will make us *do* something."

"But Tuesday's here," I countered.

"Okay yeah fine let's go."

I carefully turned around so I could climb down using the knots in the trunk as a ladder. The station wagon moved to the exit, waiting to make a left onto Central Avenue—so my soundtrack was almost over. But just as I missed my footing and fell backward, landing with a thud on the hard ground below, the wind knocked out of me, the song changed.

From his high perch, Wes looked horrified. "Dude! Are you okay?"

I couldn't speak but gave him a double thumbs-up: proof of life. He nodded and scrambled to a lower branch. As I lay there waiting for my lungs to refill, waiting for Wes to help me up and assess the damage, the new song, one I knew this time, faded into the distance as the station wagon drove away.

Turn around, bright eyes

I definitely didn't want the new kid to turn around and see me on the ground, and maybe I was concussed from the fall, but I took the song as an indication that something good was coming. Something romantic.

That's why, two years later, that song was first.

2.

TUESDAY, JULY 30, 1985

Dear Mr. Kasem,

My name is Stephanie Finnegan, but most people call me Stevie. I'm going into eighth grade at McKenna Junior High in Cheyenne, Wyoming, but first I'm leaving tomorrow for a four-week tour with the performing group I'm in, Synchronicity! I'm really excited! Anyways, I'm writing to you with a song for your Long-Distance Dedication segment.

I'd like to dedicate "Total Eclipse of the Heart" by Bonnie Tyler to my crush, Joey. I've liked him for two

years, but I think it's finally time to tell him.

Last week, after a cast party, a bunch of us snuck into the cemetery to find the legendary Green Eyes gravestone, and I was so totally freaked out by being in the graveyard at night because—I don't care if people say it's dumb—I believe in ghosts, and Joey was majorly nice to me. I grabbed on to his arm really hard when this kid Josh pretended to see a ghost behind me, and Joey didn't pull away, and he didn't laugh like his friends when I started shaking.

I heard "Total Eclipse of the Heart" the first day I met Joey, and even though it's kind of older now, it still makes so much sense for us. Like the part that talks about being terrified until she sees the look in the guy's eyes was <u>exactly</u> how I felt at the cemetery! Joey looked at me so kindly and asked me if I was okay when I was scared and even told Josh to knock it off, which was like <u>so</u> cool. And he pulled this other girl up when she tripped over a tombstone. He's so chivalrous!

I really hope you'll play my Long-Distance Dedication to Joey.

Sincerely,
Stevie Finnegan

PS: Smell the paper! I used grape ink. I hope you like it.

3.

THE CARAVAN—A borrowed Winnebago, a dented minivan, a muddy Suburban, and a trailer-lugging Bronco—pulled into the St. Francis Church parking lot in Omaha, Nebraska, a little after five in the evening. We were late: Our first performance of the tour was at seven thirty, and we only had an hour and a half to set up before costumes and makeup.

Twenty-six kids and five chaperones spilled out of the vehicles, stretching, fluffing, wiping, fanning. The chaperones were young and cool Mr. Schneider, who taught math at the high school and could do a standing backflip; Mr. and Mrs. Johnson—parents of a cast member named Amy who was a year older than me and a little scary; uptight Ms. Freeman, the professional dance

instructor, who resembled a Sorry! game piece with her round hairdo, larger bottom half, and tendency to wear all one color at a time; and Wes's mom, Margo—the only adult anyone called by her first name because she insisted on it—who was, like, basically my second mom. While the adults tried to corral the kids, the kids talked over one another and ran off to use bathrooms or gab with friends who'd been assigned to different cars. It was chaos.

I found Wes by the marquee on the church lawn.

SYNCHRONICITY PERFORMS
"A NIGHT AT THE MOVIES"
7:30 PM
ALL AGES WELCOME!

"I can't believe we're finally on tour! We're in another state!"

"I know, it's wicked!" Wes agreed, beaming. "My mom said it was in the newspaper." He smelled like bubble gum and the overpowering spicy-sweet cologne he'd started wearing. He jerked his head to the right to get his hair out of his eyes, then asked, "Have you talked to him yet?"

Like a homing missile locking on its target, I looked at Joey, who was playing hacky sack in the grass with his best friend, Shane.

In a red muscle tee and cutoffs, Joey lunged forward or backward to keep the hacky sack in the air with a knee, ankle, foot, or even his head, his shampoo-commercial hair and shark-tooth

necklace bouncing as he moved. He had catlike reflexes, especially compared to the sluggish way Shane moved. Shane whiffed, and the hacky sack dropped, making Joey laugh with his whole body, his head tipped back, guffawing toward the sky like a totally fine teen wolf.

"Stare much?" Wes laughed. "Earth to Stevie. Come in, Stevie. So, have you?"

"Have I what?"

"Talked to the dude you're drooling over right now?"

"No!" I said quickly. "It's only the first day, and the whole point of me doing the dedications is not having to actually tell him I like him but letting Casey Kasem do it! Now I just have to make it happen. And make sure every Saturday, when *American Top 40 Countdown* plays, Joey hears it."

"Huh." It was his judgmental *huh*.

"What?"

"Don't you want to be boyfriend-girlfriend with Joey?"

"Duh."

"Then don't you think you'll have to talk to him eventually?"

"Yeah, but not today," I said, sighing. "Anyways, I talk to him all the time during rehearsal—"

"When you *have* to," Wes interrupted. "When you're, like, partners."

"That's not the only time I talk to him," I said, touching my extra-curly hair and frowning. My head still itched and smelled from the chemicals.

"It's not that bad," Wes said, noticing. "And like you said, it'll relax when you wash it."

"I look like a fuzzy bowling ball," I muttered.

Wes snorted.

"Shut up!"

"You're the one who said it!"

"Yeah, but you can't laugh! Joey's seemed kind of . . . you know . . . friendlier lately, but he's never going to ask me to go with him if I have this fuzzy bowling ball head." I looked down at my oversized T-shirt and biker shorts and blew out my breath. "I don't even like this outfit."

"Why'd you wear it, then?"

"Why are you so annoying?"

Wes cracked up. "Just show Joey your awesome personality, and he'll fall in love with you."

I rolled my eyes.

"No, for reals, Stevie, I mean it," he said, softer. Adjusting one of his navy striped wristbands, he added, "You're so much nicer than most girls, especially my sisters." My cheeks started to turn pink, and he cleared his throat, raising his chin in Joey's direction. "You just gotta show him that. And you can, but only if you talk to him."

As if Wes were magic and had made it so, Shane accidentally kicked the hacky too hard, and it flew way over Joey's head, landing, like, three feet from me. I looked at the multicolored bag, then at Wes, then at Joey . . . who was jogging toward us to retrieve it.

"Now's your chance," Wes whispered excitedly. "This is awesome!"

"This is *not* awesome!" I whispered back.

"Yes, it is! Talk to him!"

"No!" My armpits were sweaty.

"Yes!" Wes hissed.

Then he was here. "Hey, guys," Joey said casually, stopping so close I could feel his exhale. "How's it going?"

I got a zap in the heart when he looked at me with eyes so dark, I couldn't see pupils.

"We're good," Wes answered, stuffing his hands in his pockets and nodding. "Just chillin'."

I nodded, too, like, a lot. I looked like a bobblehead.

"Cool beans," Joey said, "well, I'm gonna . . ."

He leaned over to pick up the hacky. My chance to talk to him was dwindling by the second. Biting my lip, I tried to think of something to say. Then I noticed that Joey only used his right pointer and middle finger to pick up the hacky, like finger chopsticks. Or like . . .

"E.T.!" I exclaimed, louder than I meant to.

Everyone within earshot was silent for a few seconds. Confused, Joey said, "Okay . . ."

Wes looked at me with his eyes wide as if to communicate, *I one hundred percent did not tell you to shout the name of a stubby alien who only knows, like, five words.*

"Did Finnegan just call you an extraterrestrial, DeLeon?"

Shane called, bursting into laughter. He wrapped his arms around his thick middle and bent forward. It wasn't *that* hilarious.

"I think so?" Joey said, laughing a little, too. Wes covered his eyes and shook his head.

"No, I meant that . . . you know how E.T. picks up . . . you know, like . . . when he follows the candy . . . and he . . ." I tried to explain, making finger chopsticks with both hands, tripping on syllables, some louder than others, some seeming like they had a death grip on the back of my throat.

"You look like a lobster," Wes muttered. I quickly dropped my hands to my sides. Then, to Joey, he said, "We were just talking about our favorite movies."

"Ohhhh!" Joey said, nodding. "That makes sense. *E.T.*'s a good one. Mine's *Beverly Hills Cop.*" He looked at Wes expectantly.

"*Indiana Jones*," Wes replied. "The first one. Obviously."

"*Terminator!*" Shane shouted from the edge of the lawn even though no one asked him. "Hurry up, dude!"

"Later," Joey said with a slight lift of his chin before jogging back to resume their game.

"That was . . ." Wes began, his words trailing off.

"Don't. Just don't." I changed the subject. "It's muggy. I wish we could go swimming."

I really wished I could go sit at the bottom of a pool for as long as my lungs allowed, blocking out the entire world. Being in water always made me feel okay. Brandon and I had both been on the swim team since we were little.

"You're, like, half human, half mer-girl," Wes said.

"I'd like to be a full mer," I said, mentally replaying the humiliation.

E.T.!

Lobster fingers!

Oh my god.

"Uh-oh," Wes said.

"What now?"

"My mom found the megapho—"

"HEY!" Margo shouted, and everyone turned to stone like they were in a giant game of freeze tag. Margo's four fellow chaperones surrounded her, looking like they meant business.

Wes and I hurried over. In her scratchy smoker's voice, Margo, leaning from side to side, long auburn hair swishing like a horse's tail, addressed the cast.

"*Everyone* is helping with setup," she said, scanning the kids in front of her, then focusing on the ones in the back, the oldest in the cast. They leaned casually against the orange-and-brown WINNEBAGO logo, looking like grown-ups with their mustaches and spiked hair and big boobs even though none of them could vote yet. "Can you hear me back there?"

A few of them nodded in agreement, sparing no precious breath for actual words.

Margo went on. "Same deal as last year and the year before. Anyone not pulling their weight cleans restrooms after the show."

Wes and I looked at each other with eyebrows raised; a few kids groaned.

"It's already quarter to six," worried Ms. Freeman, patting her teased-to-roundness hair. Her monochrome choice of the day was royal blue—she had on royal blue high waters and a matching royal blue button-up shirt. "We need to start setting up."

Ms. Freeman was here to make sure we danced as well as possible, which was probably tough since some of the kids had two left feet. But the whole point of Synchronicity was that any kid was welcome, even if they weren't coordinated or couldn't ever remember the lyrics that we lip-synched along with. Margo had made sure Synchronicity was for everyone; she founded the group after one of her daughters was told she wasn't good enough for choir.

"Okay, let's go live life with jazz hands!" Margo said.

Mr. Schneider, the chaperone who controlled the audio during the show, and who both looked and talked like a surfer despite being from Wyoming, walked over and flung open the trailer doors to start handing out props and costumes.

I avoided Joey's gaze as Wes and I got in line.

E.T.!

Lobster fingers.

Come on!

I hadn't really seen my brother much since our mom had dropped us off that morning—we weren't assigned to the same car—but Wes and I ended up in line behind him and Josh, who

everyone ironically called Little Josh since he was giant. Brandon was leaner and no short stack himself, nearly eye to eye with our six-foot-two dad now. Brandon also shared our dad's dirty blond hair, tanned skin, and blue eyes, whereas I had dark brown hair, medium brown eyes, and fair skin, like our mom.

I tapped him on the shoulder. "Bran," I said softly.

He didn't turn around; instead, he popped the collar on his polo shirt.

Assuming he hadn't heard me, I tapped him again. "Bran," I said a little louder.

He glanced over his shoulder. "Oh, hey, what's up?" He faced forward, not waiting for me to answer.

"I was just wondering if"—I pulled on his shirtsleeve—"hey, are you listening?"

He finally turned around. "What's up?"

I stepped close and did a squiggle finger to make him bend down, then asked, "Are you feeling okay?"

Brandon quickly looked around to make sure that no one was listening, then nodded tightly.

"And you took your—"

"Shh!" Brandon cut me off, quickly looking again from Wes, who was staring off into space, to Josh, who was now talking to someone else, then back at me. "I'm *fine*, Stevie," he said quietly, leaning closer. "You don't need to, like . . ." He shook his head. "You don't need to be like Mom."

The line moved forward.

I raised my eyebrows, surprised by his tone. Brandon and I had always gotten along; we rarely fought about anything. "Geez, I'm not!" I said, heat creeping up my neck. "Who peed in your Rice Krispies?"

The line moved forward again.

"I knew this was going to be weird," Brandon muttered.

"What do you mean by *that*?"

"I mean us on tour together."

"Do you, like, not *want* me here?" I shout-whispered at him.

"I don't mean it like that," he said. "Just . . . I'm okay, okay? You don't need to bring it up all the time."

My face burned. "Fine." I folded my arms over my chest.

"Hey, dude, did you see that rad comic Russell got?" Little Josh interrupted, smacking Brandon on the shoulder.

Brandon refocused on Josh.

"Huh," Wes said next to me, instantly tuned back in because of course he'd only been pretending not to listen so Brandon would keep talking. "That was strange."

"Totally," I said, feeling a gross twinge in my stomach.

I didn't say anything else because Wes and I had made it to the front of the line, and a bunch of heavy costume bags were dropped in my arms, and it was time to get ready for the first show of the tour.

4.

I FELT LIKE I was totally going to hurl.

Even though I'd performed with Synchronicity since I was five, I'd never done it in another city. It was so quiet backstage in the hallway behind the altar that I could hear the blood pounding in my ears and tiny sounds of impatient bodies around me—the swish of crinoline under a poodle skirt, the squeak of a rubber sneaker against the linoleum—as we waited for Margo to finish the introductory speech.

"Are you nervous, Stevie?"

Fifteen-year-old Christy Hutchinson's bright blue eyes were looking at me with concern.

In addition to being the best in the cast, an honor roll

student, and a seriously nice person, Christy taught step aerobics to grandmas—including mine—on the weekends at the YMCA. My grandma talked about "that sweet girl Christy" all the time. Christy was basically my idol, so this was basically humiliating.

"You're kinda green," she added, managing to look picture-perfect even with worried forehead creases. Her wavy blond hair was pulled into a high ponytail and tied with a scarf to make her look like a fifties high schooler instead of an eighties one.

"I guess," I squeaked out.

"Shh!" someone hissed from the front.

"Chill," Christy said, shaking her head. Then, to me, in a low voice, "Can I tell you a secret?" I nodded. "I still get uneasy before every show. Like, sometimes, I feel like I'll vom or space the lyrics or something."

"But . . . you . . . you've performed so long . . ."

"I know, but it's true," she whispered. "Seriously, you'll be fine by the time the chorus starts on the first song."

She put her pointer finger to her lips like she was telling me to be quiet, but then made her hand flat and set it on her other hand, which was balled into a fist, almost like paper in Rock, Paper, Scissors. "Promise," she said.

Christy sometimes did American Sign Language while she talked; her parents were both deaf.

"We're on," said someone at the front.

"Thanks, Christy," I whispered as she reached up and tightened her ponytail, a horse ready to be released from the stables.

"You got it, Stevie," she said without looking at me again. She was focused now.

The entire cast had eighteen beats of the intro to "Summer Nights" from the movie *Grease* to get into our places before the lyrics began—and we had to look chill and happy, fake gossiping with friends, but with no sound coming out of our mouths, acting nonchalant even though we were totally rushing.

Somehow, we pulled it off, the leads in front of the star boxes and the supporting cast standing around them, just in time for Christy and Trevor Buchanan to step ahead of the pack. Trevor lip-synched along with the lyrics: SUMMER LOVIN', HAD ME A BLAST, and Christy lip-synched back: SUMMER LOVIN', HAPPENED SO FAST.

They went on to lip-synch the story of their summer romance to all their "friends," just like in the movie, and by the time it got to chorus and I started lip-synching, I realized Christy had been right: I was fine. I was more than fine, actually. I was having fun. Because the thing was, I may have been a shy lobster in real life, but when a show started, I wasn't myself.

I was Performance Stevie.

And the best part of the number was coming up.

The girls were on one side of the stage, and the boys were on the other. In a few beats, the clusters blended and coupled up, then did sixteen counts of a partner dance.

My partner, thanks to our two-inch height difference, was Joey.

"Hey," he said, taking my hands in his, smiling broadly, E.T. and lobster chopsticks forgotten for the moment.

"Hey, Joey," I said warmly. Easily. Like a confident person might.

He pulled me close and switched so one hand was on my lower back and the other supported my hand near his shoulder. We stepped forward, backward, and did a ball change. He flung me to the side, making my poodle skirt fan out as I twirled, then pulled me back again like a yo-yo. He stepped behind me, his hands dropping to my waist. Right in my ear, giving me chills, he asked, "Ready, partner?"

"You know it."

At the exact same time as the other couples, Joey and I bent down, then I sprung up into a toe-touch, gaining extra height with Joey's help. The move made the audience gasp, which made me giggle.

I landed softly before Joey stepped aside. Sometimes the other boys didn't have a good hold on their dance partners and other girls stumbled on the landing—or sounded like elephants doing jumping jacks—but Joey kept a firm grip. He set me down with care every time.

He winked as we moved apart to finish the song, me smiling broadly, heart pounding, still aware of him. *Always* aware of him.

The church was packed with people, and because it wasn't dark yet and the sun was still streaming through the stained-glass windows, I could see the faces smiling back at me, so I knew they were having fun, too. And the show had only just begun!

It got even better from there.

Most of the cast rushed offstage when "Summer Nights" ended, except three girls: Christy and sisters Robyn and Courtney Rose. I lurked backstage because I didn't have a number up next. Joey was one of three boys who raced to retrieve prop typewriters from the back and set them on the tallest of the star boxes. Joey made sure Christy's prop typewriter was set up perfectly on the box. The three girls onstage each put on lensless glasses and sat down on the smallest of the star boxes, pulling them close to the tall ones to look like they were at desks.

The boys left to change, and I watched as, in perfect unison, right on the beat, Robyn, Courtney, and Christy moved their hands up and down—right, left, right, left—exaggeratedly "typing" on the typewriters until Robyn suddenly stopped, turned, and stood up while the others kept going. She effortlessly lip-synched and danced her way through the first part of the major-fast lyrics to "9 to 5" by Dolly Parton.

> *Tumble out of bed and I stumble to the kitchen*
> *Pour myself a cup of ambition . . .*

Watching them nail this number always made me happy, and I would have stayed for the whole thing, especially Christy's part, had Mrs. Johnson not beckoned me to the changing room. She wanted to know what I'd gone and done with my jumper for "It's the Hard Knock Life" from *Annie*.

We passed all nine boys in their boxing shorts and tank tops heading out of the dressing room for "Eye of the Tiger" from *Rocky*.

I tried not to melt into a puddle of Orange Crush when Joey gave me a high five as he went by.

"Need an ambulance?" Wes whispered, following the older boys.

"Break a leg, literally," I whispered before sticking out my tongue at him.

"So harsh!" he said, making a sad puppy-dog face.

"Don't really break anything," I said after him. "Just do a good job!"

"Get some crutches ready!" he called back.

"You kids," Mrs. Johnson said as we reached the changing room. "I don't know what you're talking about half the time. I do like what you've done to your hair, though, Stevie!"

Oh god.

"Thanks," I managed, making my way to my pile of costume bags. I had the combined length of the end of "9 to 5" and all of "Eye of the Tiger" and "Fame" to change. That was basically forever. I shrugged into my next costume, which Mrs. Johnson insisted on ironing first, and turned myself into an orphan who lived through the Great Depression.

I put away my "Summer Nights" costume, then hung up a few other people's costumes that'd been draped on furniture or discarded on the floor.

As I applied brown face powder meant to look like dirt, I mentally went over the choreography, especially the part where I had to go from siting on my knees to standing and back down

again in a quick *one, two, three, four* before rolling over and kicking my legs up, all without missing a beat.

My solo was the part sung by the youngest orphan. I lip-synched:

SANTA CLAUS WE NEVER SEE

Before Tuesday, who played Annie, lip-synched:

SANTA CLAUS, WHAT'S THAT? WHO'S HE?

It was the raddest performance of "It's the Hard Knock Life" I'd ever done. I skipped off the stage afterward. Then six of the older kids performed "Stayin' Alive" from *Saturday Night Fever*, and the show was half-over.

At intermission, Wes waved me to a corner of the dressing room that was partly obscured by a stack of folding chairs. We crawled behind the chairs and sat crisscross applesauce facing each other.

"What's up?" I asked. "You look serious as a heart attack."

"I did something," he admitted. "It's probably bad. No, it's *definitely* bad."

"What is it? And when did you even have time to do this bad something?"

"During *Saturday Night Fever*? When you asked me to help organize costumes, but I said I had to poop?"

"You know, you don't really always need to tell m—"

"I wasn't pooping."

"Good to know," I said, looking away for a second, embarrassed. "So if you weren't"—I waved my hand in his general direction—"then what were you doing?"

"Well, you know how I always tell you I'm going to tell Tuesday I like her, too?"

"Uh-huh," I said. "And how you always chicken out?"

He twisted his lips, hesitating.

"Holy guacamole, what did you do?" I asked, leaning forward, grabbing his forearms. Wes was almost never quiet; it was alarming.

"I was inspired by you with Joey and stuff, and I decided to make sure I really went through with it this time, especially since you already sent a letter to Casey Kasem and everything."

"I'm going to send one every single day. I brought thirty stamped envelopes that are, like, already addressed and everything. I'm going to dedicate the same song sometimes, then change it to a different song sometimes, but just keep sending them all th—"

"Hey!"

"Sorry, my bad! Tell me what you did."

"You know, people would be amazed by how much you talk when you're on a roll."

I stared at him, lips pursed. "Just tell me, okay?"

He sucked in his breath and held it, then with the exhale, his words came tumbling out. "I used the church phone to leave a message on Tuesday's answering machine, telling her that I like her and want her to be my girlfriend."

His expression looked surprised, like this was the first time he'd heard about this.

"You left the message on her answering machine at *home?*" I asked, confused.

Wes nodded, his hair falling into his eyes. He shook it out like he was annoyed with it. "She has her own phone line."

"Wow," I said, impressed. No one I knew had their own phone line. Every kid I knew had to argue over phone time with their siblings. With three older sisters, Wes could barely get two minutes of phone time a day. "But she won't hear it until we get back."

"That's the point!" Wes said, gesturing wildly. "I did it so there was no way I could back out! Now I have to tell her!" He smacked himself in the forehead.

"But you were going to tell her anyway," I said. "You said so a hundred times. You were just working up to it."

"I know, but now I *really* have to!"

We stared at each other, neither knowing what to say, until we both burst out laughing, prompting a few castmates to peer over the chairs, wondering what was so funny. Then Christy asked if I knew who hung up her costume for her, and I shrugged because I was embarrassed about it, and Margo came in to give us a five-minute warning for the second half of the show.

"It'll be okay," I whispered to Wes. "If she doesn't like you, she's missing out."

"Thanks, Stevie."

From "The NeverEnding Story" to "Ghostbusters" to "Footloose" to the two finale numbers, the second half was just as

perfect as the first. The donation top hats overflowed. My cheeks hurt from smiling. And after our final bow, completely high on adrenaline, we bounced back to the dressing room, ready to pack it all up again.

The tour had officially begun.

5.

I SNUCK AWAY and stuck another Long-Distance Dedication in the slot marked OUTGOING MAIL at a church in Des Moines, Iowa, after a performance that was just as rad as the one in Omaha. Then, only the second day of August, we were already on to Chicago.

We didn't have tons of time before setup, but Margo decided we could take an hour to kick off our shoes and run around in the sand by Lake Michigan. Like a dog off his leash, Wes was ready to bolt the second the caravan stopped.

"Go ahead, I'll catch up—I gotta go," I told him, doing a pee dance.

"Go in the water," he said, rolling his eyes.

"I'm not even in a swimsuit," I said, rolling mine back. "I'm not, like, peeing my shorts."

He shrugged and ran off.

Margo let me use the miniature bathroom in the Winnie. When I came out, I found her at the kitchenette table sorting papers and a pile of money, one pencil tucked in her auburn bun and another in her hand, forehead scrunched, mouth turned down.

"Hey, Stevie Bea," she said, face brightening when she saw me. "All set?"

I nodded, sliding into the booth, the familiar combination of coconut lotion and cigarette smoke wafting across the table. "Aren't you coming? I think, like, even Mrs. Johnson is going in the water—probably only to make sure Amy doesn't drown, but still."

Margo let loose her loud laugh that could startle you if you weren't ready for it; everyone knew Mrs. Johnson was way overprotective.

"You're a crack-up," she said, her voice scratchy and comforting like a wool sweater in the winter.

I blushed and looked down at my lap. Margo reached across the table and covered my hand with hers. "Everything okay so far? It's your first big tour!"

I nodded, feeling as relaxed around Margo as I did around my own mom—they were friends, so it was like my mom had passed the parental torch to Margo this month. Back at home,

when I wasn't at my house, I was at Wes's, burning the roof of my mouth off on a freezer potpie that Margo had heated up in a hurry because she hadn't had time to cook dinner.

"No homesickness? Missing your parents? Your own bed?" she asked, keeping her soft hand on mine. Margo had a way of making you feel like you were the only person in the world.

"We only just left."

"There's no timetable on feelings, sweetie." She let go and picked up a piece of notebook paper. "Just promise to find me if you need anything. Or if you think that son of mine who never talks to his mama needs help." She winked.

"I will," I said, smiling as I slid out of the booth, not wanting to miss my chance at the beach. I gestured toward the door. "You're really not coming?"

"No, I gotta make sure we have enough money to make it to the next stop," Margo said.

"Um," I said, instantly worried.

"I'm kidding, Stevie Bea, go have fun! Live life with jazz hands!"

I laughed at her signature saying as I jumped from the Winnie to the sidewalk, then sprinted across the sand, carelessly kicking off my shoes mid-run, one here and one way over there, before sloshing through the water toward Wes.

"What took you so long?" he asked. "You missed Little Josh and Shane trying to push each other over into the water."

"I was talking to your mom. Who won?"

"See for yourself." Wes gestured toward a huddle of boys; Little Josh and Shane both looked like drowned rats, their clothes dripping from collars to cutoffs, Josh's shirt clinging to his chest and Shane's to his belly.

I laughed. "Seems like that worked out well for both of them. Wow, Shane looks pissed."

"Doesn't he always?"

"Yeah. Sometimes I don't get why Joey picked him as his best friend."

"Maybe he's happier in private," Wes said. "Sometimes people act different when other people are around." He looked at me pointedly.

"Shut up," I said, bumping him.

He touched the side of his head to my shoulder, to say without saying he loved me the way I was, even if I was a motormouth around him that lost the ability to speak around many others.

Next to each other, Wes and I took in our surroundings. It was surreal to stand there with cool, turquoise lake water up to my thighs, vibrant green space beyond the sun-scorched beach, skyscrapers for miles in the distance.

I thought of how, in just one window in just one of those buildings, there was a single person doing something, talking on the phone or doing chores or listening to tapes, and it blew my mind a little.

"Maybe I'll move to a big city someday," I said.

"We could be roommates and get an aquarium like they have at the dentist," Wes replied. The hems of his tan shorts were dark brown because they were soaked. I was taller, so mine were dry.

"I don't want our apartment to look like a dentist office," I said, touching the end of my French braid. "But maybe we can have a small fishbowl."

"And I'll have a betta fish named Reginald."

"I thought your D&D character was Reginald."

"There can be more than one Reginald in the world. Tuesday and I are also naming our firstborn child Reginald. Reginald Mortimer Savage. *Killer.*"

"You might want to tell her you like her before making that decision," I said, laughing.

"I'm getting to it," Wes assured me.

Then, too soon, Margo yelled that it was time to go.

AFTER OUR PERFORMANCE at the Masonic Temple, the third show of the tour's twenty-two, we were assigned to stay with host families for the first time. The families were people who had signed up to take small groups of us home and let us sleep in their spare rooms or attics in exchange for reserved seats at the show.

I was glad we wouldn't have to roll out sleeping bags on a

hard church basement floor again, but I was kinda weirded out by the idea of going home with total strangers—after being told explicitly my entire life *not* to go home with strangers.

Megaphone in hand, swaying back and forth as usual, Margo called names like bingo numbers, pairing host families with their small groups of Synchronicity cast members—usually no more than five per house. Up close in the bright lobby, the families got to see our true postshow faces, scarred by pesky and persistent stage makeup. Here and there were red-stained lips, a single heavily lined eye, a gob of foundation in a hairline. We looked like toddlers who'd been playing in their mothers' bathroom vanities.

The other chaperones were doing rounds through the church and the dressing room, making sure we hadn't left anything, or anyone, behind.

Margo assigned me to a family called the Davises. I was relieved when she called Brandon's name, too. Amy Johnson's bingo number was up next, and then I almost died.

"Did she just say Joey?" I whispered urgently to Wes. "Are Joey and I staying at the same host house?"

"She definitely said Joey," Wes said, nodding and smiling. "It's your lucky day! Maybe I'll get to stay with Tuesday!"

"It's my unlucky day! Joey will see my Pegasus pajamas!"

"Who cares?" Wes asked, nudging me. "Now you can, like, *talk* to him. But in a normal way. Just stick to topics that, you know, make sense."

"You're so funny I forgot to laugh."

Margo was signaling for me to hurry up and go stand by the Davis family, so I hoisted my overstuffed duffel onto my shoulder, hugged Wes goodbye, and slowly weaved through the crowd. Mr. and Mrs. Davis were telling Amy and Joey what "great singers" we all were and their bored-looking son rolled his eyes and said we'd only lip-synched the whole time.

Joey kept looking at himself in the reflection in the window, messing with his excellently feathered hair. He was so cute!

I sidled up next to Brandon, who was nearby but not part of the conversation.

"Hey," I said super quietly, bugged by the Davis kid's comment.

"Hey, Steves," he said before lifting his chin in the kid's direction. "Don't let him tick you off. Some people don't get it and that's cool. Most people do." He nudged me and gestured at the kid's pristine Air Jordans.

"Holy moly," I whispered. "Are you jealous?"

"I might steal them," he joked. "It looks like we're about the same shoe size."

"It's about time you kicked off your life of crime," I joked back, happy he was being normal. "This good kid act is getting boring. Remember that time you returned the ten bucks you found outside the movie theater?"

"You would have done the same," he said, rubbing the back of his neck.

"I would have taken it to the arcade," I said confidently. Brandon rolled his eyes, knowing I'd have given the money back, too.

After everyone got their assignments, our group piled into the wayback of the Davises' maroon station wagon and left the twinkling lights of the city and the rest of the cast behind. I tried not to be jealous when Amy sleepily rested her head on Joey's shoulder—everyone was always doing that on tour. I wanted to be the only one with my head on Joey's shoulder.

Thankfully, it wasn't too long until we ended up at a house on a street that reminded me of ours at home, just with way more trees and less elbow room between the houses.

Mrs. Davis served us meat lasagna and iceberg lettuce salad with ranch dressing, then showed us to our rooms for the night. There were sleeping bags rolled out for Brandon and Joey on the floor in the family room, and Amy and I got the guest bedroom.

Mrs. Davis closed the door behind her, and immediately Amy turned toward me, her glossy black hair flying out, then settling perfectly in place. "I like horror stories, but I don't want to *sleep* in one."

Nodding slowly, I took in the largest porcelain doll collection I'd ever seen. "It *is* a lotta dolls . . . for, um, people who don't, um, you know, like, have any daughters."

"It's a lotta dolls for *anyone*," Amy responded in her superfast way of talking, where there were barely breaks between the words. "I wonder if the Davises are axe murderers."

Goose bumps grew on my bare arms as my gaze snagged on an extra creepy doll over Amy's twin bed, with one eye pointing up and the other pointing to the side.

"Mrs. Johnson likes porcelain dolls, but she has, like, five," Amy said. "And they're in the basement, where all doll collections should be."

I wanted her to stop talking about the dolls. "Why do you, um, call your mom Mrs. Johnson?"

"I don't to her face. And besides, isn't that what you call her?" Amy raised one eyebrow, a skill I hadn't been able to master.

"Yeah, but . . ." I was getting more and more stressed out by the conversation; my volume dropped, and the words got stuck on my tonsils. "I'm . . . She's not my mom," I sputtered. Amy was Joey's age, a year older than me, and every conversation with her felt like an argument.

"She's not my mom, either," she said.

"But . . ." I could feel my face heating up. "She's your . . . The Johnsons adopted you when you were a baby."

Amy's mouth dropped open in surprise. She covered it and asked through her hand, "How do you know I'm adopted?"

I took a step back, the frilly comforter on the twin bed behind me tickling the backs of my knees. "Um, because . . . you . . . they . . . you were . . . born in China . . ." My words trailed off.

Amy didn't say anything for a second, then suddenly busted

up. "I'm just joshing you, Stevie! Chill out! Everyone knows I'm adopted." She shook her head. "I just call my mom Mrs. *Johnson* when I'm annoyed at her, like I am right now, because she, like, took away my copy of *Cujo* because some lady at the church in Des Moines told her it was too scary for a fourteen-year-old, and it's totally not!" She folded her arms over her chest. "Dude, you look so totally stressed! Chill out!"

"Okay," I said, turning to face the bed, trying to regroup by unpacking my pajamas and toiletries. "I mean, I'm fine. It's just . . . it's hot in here."

"I guess so," Amy said even though it totally wasn't.

Amy collapsed on her bed and muttered, "These dolls are way scarier than the dog in *Cujo*."

Exhausted from the conversation, the performance, and not much sleep the night before, I took my supplies and went to the bathroom to get ready for bed. Afterward, I found the Davis adults playing cards at the kitchen table.

"Um, excuse me?"

"Oh, hello, uh . . ." Mrs. Davis began.

"Stevie," I said.

"That's right, Stevie," she said. "Such an unusual name for a girl. Is everything all right?"

"Oh yes," I said, shifting my weight. "I'm just wondering if, um, you could maybe, um, mail a letter for me tomorrow? I wouldn't ask, um, but it's, like, mega important."

"Well, if it's *mega* important," Mr. Davis said with a chuckle, "I'm happy to mail it for you, Stevie. I'm going into the office tomorrow, and my route takes me right by the main post office downtown. Give it here." He extended the hand not holding a fan of cards.

I pulled the stamped envelope from my toiletry case and gave it to Mr. Davis, hoping I could trust him to remember to mail the letter in the morning.

"Thank you," I said, hesitating. "And thank you for letting us stay here."

"You're welcome, dear, it's our pleasure. Anything else you need?" Mrs. Davis smiled, but her face told me to skedaddle.

"That's it, good night," I said.

"Good night!" the Davises enthusiastically replied in unison. I heard Mr. Davis ask, "Whose turn was it?" as I made my way back to the guest bedroom.

Amy was already asleep with the light on, so I flipped the switch and climbed into bed, trying hard not to think of all the little eyes watching me in the dark.

At two in the morning, still wide awake, I crept to the now empty kitchen for a glass of water. I wanted to call home, but it was the middle of the night and the long-distance call would cost the Davises money. I tried to shove away homesickness by noticing the things that were similar: the cool linoleum beneath my bare feet; the thick plastic cups that suctioned together so

tightly you had to yank them apart; the sound of the sprinklers *tick-tick-tiiiiiiiiiick*ing in the dark night.

I finished my water and set the cup in the sink. As I turned toward the hallway, a silhouette appeared, making me gasp. Joey stepped into the sliver of moonlight in the kitchen doorway, panic on his face.

"Stevie, there's something wrong with Brandon. He's—"

"Move," I cut him off, shoving past Joey and rushing into the family room.

The lights were out, but I could make out the lump of Brandon clenching and contorting inside his sleeping bag and hear the familiar wet, strangled sound that his mouth made when his brain went haywire.

I dropped hard to my knees next to my brother.

"I don't know what happ—"

"Help me turn him," I interrupted.

"What?" Joey asked, hesitating. "Shouldn't we wake up the Davises so they can, like, take him to the emergency room?"

"No, just come down here and help me!" I commanded. Joey crouched next to me, and together we gently rolled Brandon onto his right side so he wouldn't swallow his tongue. I made sure his pillow was supporting his head.

"It's okay," I murmured quietly. The shaking was already slowing.

"It doesn't seem okay," Joey said. "Shouldn't we call an ambulance?"

"Did it start right before you came to the kitchen?" I asked. Joey nodded, worry all over his face. "Then no, we don't need to," I said. "See, it's stopping. It's a short one." Even though the tremors were slowing, I kept a firm hand on Brandon's left shoulder, the other against his back. "This wasn't too bad."

"This has happened before?" Joey asked. "What's wrong with him?"

I looked at him sharply. "Nothing's *wrong* with him, Joey, he has epilepsy." Brandon had stopped shaking, but he wasn't aware of us yet. "It's just something that happens sometimes. It's a reaction in his brain that makes his body shake. It doesn't happen all that often, and he takes medicine for it. But sometimes it does."

"That's, like . . . *whoa*," Joey said. I noticed he still had his hands pressed against Brandon, too: one behind his knee and the other behind his ankle. Joey started chattering a mile a minute. "Wow, Stevie, you really knew what to do; you're good at this. I don't know what I'd have done if you weren't in the kitchen. I, like, didn't know what was happening. Like I had no idea Brandon was, like . . ."

"You can't tell anyone." I filled in his pause quickly, thinking of how Brandon had snapped at me when I'd tried to ask him how he was feeling. "He's, like, really embarrassed about it. I didn't know that he hadn't told anyone, but I guess no one knows. And . . ."

"What?"

"Our parents were afraid to send him on tour this time because it got kinda worse over the school year," I admitted. "The doctor adjusted his medication, but still, if our parents knew he had a seizure, they might make him go home."

"Wouldn't that be, like, better or whatever?" Joey asked. "So he could get better at home?"

"He's not sick," I said testily.

"I know, but I mean, like, get help. Isn't it better to be around your parents so they could help him?"

"No," Brandon answered, startling me and Joey. "They're overprotective. Even the doctor said it was okay for me to go on tour." His words were a little slurred, but not that bad.

"Welcome back," I said, squeezing his shoulder.

"I did my signature dance moves, huh?" Brandon asked, carefully rolling to his back, then easing up to a sitting position. We helped him until he was leaning against the couch.

"Dude," Joey said once Brandon was upright. "That was . . ."

"Yeah," Brandon said, rubbing his head, blinking back into reality.

"You're lucky your sister was here," Joey said, shaking jitters out of his hands. He sounded like he'd eaten a bunch of sugar. "I was, like, totally clueless. I mean, for reals, I did *not* know what to do."

"Yeah," Brandon said, half smiling at me. His eyes snapped back to Joey. "Don't tell anyone, okay?"

Joey nodded. "Stevie already told me—I won't."

I went and got Brandon some water, then told Joey he could go to sleep, but that I was going to stick around for a while to make sure Brandon was okay.

"You could move your sleeping bag over there, and we could turn off the lamp?" I offered.

"Nah, I'm good," Joey said, moving toward the built-in bookcase. "I don't sleep much anyway." He had on gray sweat shorts, a light blue muscle tee, and gym socks—one with yellow stripes and one with navy. I laughed. "What?" he asked, turning around.

"Your socks don't match. I've never seen you in mismatched socks."

He looked at his feet, then slowly back at me, a smile building on his lips. "Do you pay a lot of attention to my socks, Finnegan?"

My earlobes got hot, but my brother saved me.

"She's totally observant," he said. "Hey, man, get a game or something to pass the time."

"Monopoly?" Joey asked, facing the bookshelf and stretching, exposing patches of black armpit hair.

"Worst game ever," Brandon said. "Is there Trivial Pursuit? I'm awesome at trivia." He still sounded out of it.

"That'll take all night," I protested, watching Joey run a long, thin finger down the sides of the game boxes.

"How about Scrabble?" Joey asked.

Brandon and I agreed, and Joey pulled the box out from the stack on the shelf, bringing it over to the coffee table. When Joey

went to see if there were any sodas in the fridge, I tipped toward Brandon and asked, "Are you sure you're okay?"

"*Psha*, for sure," he said, waving it off. "It was a child-sized one, not a granddaddy. Don't worry so much, okay?" He ruffled my hair, and I shoved him away, smoothing my curls before Joey came back.

"It's diet, but it'll do the trick," Joey said. He stared right into my eyes when he handed me the soda, our fingers brushing with the exchange. Once he was settled around the table with us, he said, "I'll go first."

Brandon smirked at me, and I knew what he was thinking, that if *he'd* just announced that he was going first, I'd have pointed out that it was against the rules—and the only reason I didn't was because it was Joey.

I shrugged at my brother because he was right.

Joey went; his word was *socks*. We all busted up.

"Seemed appropriate since you're so fascinated by them," Joey said, making Brandon cough-laugh.

"You wish," I retorted, surprising myself. After checking my tiles, using the *O* in socks, I spelled the word *cocky*.

"Oh, I see how it is!" Joey said, eyes on his tiles, muttering, "Stevie Finnegan is not messing around." He picked up a letter.

"Dude, it's my turn." Brandon frowned.

"Oh right, right," Joey said.

Brandon played *yacked*, and there was a mini argument about whether it was slang or a real word, and then Joey's eyes lit up when he checked his tileboard again.

"Radical!" he murmured, adding an *M* above the *A*, pausing to smile up at me, then setting down the *T, C,* and *H* tiles. He winked before taking a sip of his soda.

My stomach flipped when I read the word: *match*. Though I knew he was probably still referring to socks, a part of me wondered if a part of Joey might have meant us.

That maybe we, me and him, could be a match, too. Mismatched but still cute, just like his socks.

Brandon's mega-loud yawn startled me from my thoughts.

"You guys, I know you mean well, but I'm ready to hit the hay," he said. "This Scrabble game is so boring, I'm basically, like, already asleep."

"Harsh, man," Joey joked, adding, "no worries."

"Totally, you should sleep," I said, standing up quickly and dumping the game pieces back in the box. The clock on the wall said it was after three in the morning. Just seeing that made me sleepy, too.

I told them both good night and crept into the hall.

"Hey," Joey whispered after me. "What if . . ." He looked worried about being left alone with Brandon. He rubbed his hands on his shorts.

"Come get me if anything else happens," I said. "I know what to do."

Joey nodded. "Okay, but what if, like, I don't hear it and wake up."

"Impossible."

"Okay," he nodded again. "Yeah, yeah, you're right. Okay." He sighed, seeming reassured, then gave me a small smile. "You really do know what to do. You're a good sister, Stevie, it's rad. And don't worry, I'll keep his secret. Swear I won't tell anyone."

"Not even Shane?" I asked, tipping my head and folding my arms over my chest.

Joey laughed a little. "Especially not Shane! That kid can't keep a secret to save his life. He accidentally ratted me out to my grandma once when I told her I wasn't the one who left the gate open after the dog ran away."

Horrified, I asked, "Did you get your dog back?"

Joey's face turned gooey-sweet. "Oh yeah, Molly came home. She's a good girl."

"Awesome," I whispered, shifting from one bare foot to the other in the dark hallway, liking Joey's obvious love for his dog, suddenly aware of my braless state and wondering if my sleep-bun had morphed into a sleep-porcupine. "Well . . ."

"Well," Joey repeated. The tone of his voice felt almost . . . flirty?

The confidence I'd had during the crisis with Brandon melted away like an iceberg in a frying pan, and what was left was just plain old me, standing in Pegasus pajamas in front of the boy I'd had a crush on for two years, who had maybe, possibly been flirting with me tonight.

Mouth dry as a desert, lasagna and ranch dressing rolling around in my stomach, I felt like it was suddenly all too much.

"Good night, Joey," I said abruptly.

He looked surprised. "Good night?"

"Go check on my brother!" I bossed, wanting to be away from him so I could think about what had happened when we were together.

"Okay, okay!" Joey replied, holding up his hands. "See you in the morning."

As soon as Joey was gone, I crept back to bed and climbed under the covers, careful not to wake up Amy.

I went to sleep alternating between worrying about Brandon and being happy about unexpected time with Joey—and wondering how I was going to get him to listen to the radio the next morning.

After all, tomorrow was Saturday—the day *American Top 40 Countdown* aired each week and the first opportunity for Joey to hear one of my Long-Distance Dedications.

6.

THE HOST FAMILIES returned the dispersed Synchronicity stars to the Masonic Temple Saturday morning. My eyes burned from lack of sleep, but I was buzzing with energy because *American Top 40 Countdown* would air soon—and with it, my chance to tell Joey how I felt.

After roll call, the chaperones left to gas up the vehicles, which they hadn't done earlier because Margo had all the donation money, and I guess they'd stayed in different places—who knows where. While we waited, most kids in the cast amused themselves by playing a version of human chess using the temple's checkerboard floor.

The very oldest kids, the mysterious sixteen-and-seventeen-

year-olds, vegged in a dark corner, draped over duffels, rolled-up sleeping bags, and one another like beautiful dead bodies.

Wes and I sat on the steps of the stage we'd performed on last night.

"We have to be in the same car with him when it airs," Wes said. "That's the only way we can make sure he's listening."

"But the show's four hours long, and we don't know when the Long-Distance Dedication will play!" I said, eyes on Joey. He was standing on two different dark gray tiles, paying attention to the game but also looking over his shoulder every once in a while at Brandon—like he was checking on him—then at me, zapping me in the heart every time. "Mr. Schneider said Cleveland is five hours away. You know the Chicago radio station will cut out at some point! What if it plays then and we miss it?"

"We'll pick up the Cleveland radio station," Wes said, scratching his forehead under his headband, then snorting. "She's Frogger." Tuesday hopped across the tiles, dodging other kids like they were cars on the street.

"Focus!"

"Sorry!" He paused, then asked, "Aren't there any cities between Chicago and Cleveland?"

"How would I know?" I asked. "Do I look like a road atlas?"

"We need a new plan."

Wes turned his attention to one of his three older sisters, the meanest of the twins: Kris. In looks only, Kris was an older, taller, girl version of Wes, with the same smooth olive skin,

medium brown hair, and kind brown eyes—which made it ironic that she was such a demon. We watched as Kris attempted to shove Christy off her light gray tile, cheating since the game was supposed to be no contact.

"We need to stay here, at least until the Long-Distance Dedication airs," Wes said. "That's the only way we'll be sure he hears it."

"I know, but the chaperones will be back soon. And the Winnie's already gassed up outside. There's, like, no way they'll let us hang around here that long."

"Unless they have no choice," Wes said, a gleam in his eye.

"You're disqualified for rough play!" Little Josh yelled at Kris after Kris successfully pushed Christy over. Kris held her middle finger in Josh's face as Christy dusted herself off and resumed the game, telling Kris to "chill already."

"Hey, Kris, come here," Wes called, waving her over.

She rolled her eyes but came over anyway. "What do you nerds want?" She rested her hands on her hips and looked at us expectantly. I liked her red-and-white dolphin shorts but didn't tell her; speaking to Kris was dangerous, even if you had something nice to say. Wes was the only person who wasn't afraid of her.

"We need a favor," he said.

Kris tsked and rolled her eyes again. "Oh, do you?"

"Yeah, and you're gonna do it because I'll do your chores for a month when we get home."

"Even the lawn?" Kris asked, tipping her head to the side.

The front yard at their house had a steep hill that no one liked to mow for fear of death by lawn mower.

"Even the lawn." Wes nodded sharply. He may have been only thirteen and small in stature, but he was a cunning negotiator.

"What would I need to do?" Kris asked.

"Keep us here until noon," Wes said. "By any means necessary." He paused before adding, "Except death. Don't kill anyone."

"As if," Kris said, laughing. "Why in the world do you want... You know, never mind, I don't even want to know what goes on in your nerdy little brains." After a surprisingly short pause, she shrugged her tan shoulders and said, "Okay."

"Really?" Wes and I asked in unison.

"Sure, why not," she said. "I'm bored, and it's always fun to mess with Mom." She tapped a finger to her bottom lip. "Let's see, should I let out the air of the Winnie's tires? Should I suddenly have a medical emergency? Ooh, this is going to be fun!"

An hour and a half later, Margo paced the Masonic Temple like a caged tiger. Mr. Schneider was trying to teach some of the boys how to do a backflip, and the Johnsons had left to fetch food. Groups of kids were sprawled here and there, the human chess game forgotten.

After assuring us that what she'd done wouldn't permanently harm anyone, but not telling us what it was to protect the

innocent, Kris had popped a squat next to her fraternal twin, Holly, and passed out with the rest of the dark-corner corpses.

Wes, Tuesday, Amy, Joey, Shane, Christy, Little Josh, Brandon, and I all sat in a blurry circle around Little Josh's boom box, playing I Never while listening to *American Top 40 Countdown* in the background. The plan had worked perfectly—for everyone except uptight Ms. Freeman, the yellow Sorry! game piece today in her bright yellow sundress, who had rushed to the restroom in a hurry after sipping from a coffee cup left out for the chaperones.

My guilt about her discomfort came and went depending on how close Joey's knee was to touching mine at any given moment.

"You're up, Finnegan," he said, bumping me, making my heart thump. Quietly, he added, "Like my socks? I wore them just for you."

He had on the same mismatched pair as last night. I ignored the grossness of him rewearing dirty socks and focused on the fact that he'd done it deliberately . . . for *me*. I got an instant fever.

"Go, Stevie," Brandon said.

"Oh . . . uh . . . um . . . I never . . . swam in Blue Lake," I managed to spit out.

"Really?" Christy asked, leaning forward so she could see me around Joey. She raised her hand to indicate that she had.

"No way," Joey said, raising a hand, too. Casey Kasem announced number twenty-eight in the countdown, "Would I Lie to You?" by Eurythmics. "This song is gnarly."

"Sooo good," Tuesday replied, before asking me, "You've

never even done the rope swing?" She'd recently shaved one side of her chin-length, light red hair, and earrings lined her visible ear, lobe to point. She looked radical.

I shook my head. "She's afraid of leeches," Brandon said, embarrassing me.

"Am not," I quietly protested, my cheeks still hot. I plucked at my shirt to cool myself down.

"She totally is," he said to Little Josh, and the two of them laughed.

I was surprised by the teasing, but I let it go because I knew Brandon was probably out of it from the seizure and not sleeping much last night—he had bags under his eyes to prove it. I wanted to ask him if he felt okay and had remembered to take his medicine, but we'd been around other people all morning.

"Everyone's afraid of leeches," Christy chimed in. "Barf me out!"

"I think they're cool," Shane said before burping for five seconds straight.

After people gagged and fanned their noses and told Shane he was so grody, Tuesday turned to me again. Smiling with her whole freckle-speckled face, she said, "Stevie, you should come with me and Amy sometime. The rope swing is the best. Right, Amy?"

"Sure," Amy said, monotone. She was dressed entirely in black—black tank top, black biker shorts, black high-tops—like she was in mourning for her confiscated horror novel.

I could feel Wes's excitement, but I couldn't look at him or I'd

fully turn into a tomato. I knew he was thrilled on two levels—that I'd gotten an invitation to do something with a person other than him, and that the person was his beloved Tuesday—and surely, he'd want to tag along. But I knew it'd never happen. I knew Tuesday was just being nice because she was always nice to everyone. That's just how people were, nice to my face to be polite but not really wanting to be friends. It was like when Jennifer from across the street at home said she would invite me to her birthday party, but . . .

I never got an invitation to Jennifer T.'s birthday party.

I never watched Jennifer T.'s mom decorate their front porch, wondering if I should show up anyway.

I never cried while counting how many girls showed up at Jennifer T.'s party—how many girls had *received their invitations.*

I shook my head to clear it like a mental Etch A Sketch. A few more people took their turns at I Never, and I played along, acting copacetic, but the farther Casey Kasem got into the countdown, the more my blood pressure rose. I felt like my heart was going to jump out of my chest every time a song ended, thinking the Long-Distance Dedication was up next.

And then it was.

Everyone got quiet, listening. Apparently, I wasn't the only one who loved this part best.

"This week's Long-Distance Dedication comes from . . ." Casey Kasem began. Wes and I locked eyes.

". . . a girl . . ."

Our eyes widened in unison.

". . . named Megan in Nevada. Megan writes . . ."

I hadn't realized I'd been holding my breath until it gushed out of me like a popped balloon. Brandon took his turn at I Never and said he'd never had stitches, and Amy and Joey raised their hands, and across the circle, Wes and I locked eyes again. He mouthed, "Sorry."

I half smiled and shrugged, like I wasn't disappointed, but I was.

In the periphery, I could have sworn that Christy had noticed the exchange, but when I looked at her, she was focused on her fingernails, so I must have been wrong.

Casey Kasem introduced the next song in the countdown, and as the keyboard intro began, Joey shifted so his bare knee was even closer to mine, our body heat trapped between us.

How can I convince you

Joey casually leaned back, planting his palms flat on the floor behind him, his nearest thumb an inch from mine. He smelled like deodorant and the host family's flowery soap and something else unidentifiable, warm and *him*. I was unaware of anything but the song and the sound of Joey's breath.

What you see is real?

Laser beams of liking shot out of me, and I swore I felt them back from Joey. He wasn't really playing the game anymore, either. I wondered if he was listening to the lyrics, feeling my

lasers, wondering if maybe, just maybe, I was more interesting than he'd thought.

I was so into the song that I literally screamed when Margo shouted, "TIME TO GO," into the megaphone. Wes laughed so hard he crumpled to the ground and tears streamed out of his eyes, which made Tuesday, Amy, Brandon, and Christy laugh, too.

Already on his feet, Joey held out a hand and pulled me up. "All right, there, Finnegan?" he said, smirking.

"Yeah," I said quietly. "I was just into the song."

"You have good taste," he said.

Always a gentleman, Joey helped Christy up, then Tuesday, too, before jogging off to find Shane and leaving me wondering if Joey and I had just had, like, a real, honest-to-god *moment*.

7.

SATURDAY, AUGUST 3, 1985

Dear Mr. Kasem,

How are you? I'm fine. My name is Stevie Finnegan, and I'm writing to dedicate a song to a boy I like. We're in a performing group together. I already sent some dedications, and they didn't make this week's show, but that's okay because I have an even better one now!

I'd like to dedicate "The Search Is Over" by Survivor to Joey. We bonded over something kinda intense, and I think maybe Joey might see me different now. The whole song is about taking someone for granted but

then realizing they're awesome! And there's a line that talks about how the highway's like leading him back to her. I think that's rad because Joey and I are on a tour together, and at the end, we'll take the highway back home, and hopefully be together.

Sincerely,
Stevie Finnegan

PS: Can you smell the cherry ink? I think it's my favorite.

8.

JUST WHEN WE thought we could do no wrong on tour, we performed at a community center in Cleveland.

Only a few seconds into "Summer Nights," Shane tripped and, while sprawled on the floor, accidentally tripped Christy. Shane was fine, but Christy twisted her ankle, so she had to sit out the rest of the show.

Kris was the understudy on "9 to 5," but she hadn't rehearsed it recently, because she was always late to practice due to staying out past curfew every night, so she forgot a bunch of the dance steps, then got frustrated and walked offstage *in the middle of the song.*

"Uh, Kris?" I asked as she stormed by me.

"A hurricane's coming," Wes muttered as he watched his mom's eyes widen to near-cartoon-popping-out proportions.

"Kristine Marie Savage!" Margo hissed, trailing her daughter with smoke pouring out of her ears.

The next few numbers were okay, but then Little Josh couldn't find his costume for "The NeverEnding Story" so he had to do the number in his seventies outfit from "Stayin' Alive," which didn't really fit with the flying dragon vibe. It was easy to see the confusion on the audience members' faces, because it was the middle of the day and they were sitting in folding chairs that started about ten feet in front of us.

In the end, Margo didn't pass the top hats. Wes and I were convinced she was going to kill us all, but instead we went out for pizza and all made a pact that we'd never speak of Cleveland again.

9.

SUNDAY, THE END of the first (short) week, we had a free day at Niagara Falls. There weren't thirty-one tickets available for the Maid of the Mist boat ride that takes you on the water, so we went to the Cave of the Winds in Niagara State Park.

In batches, we rode the elevator down one hundred and seventy-five feet into the gorge, packed like sardines. Joey was squished against the wall, and I ended up right in front of him. I was positive he could hear my heartbeat even though his ears were probably pressurized like mine as the elevator dropped to what felt like the center of Earth.

I had a bright yellow poncho over my clothes; I looked ridiculous.

"Hey, Finnegan," Joey said, "your hair smells good. Like a Jolly Rancher."

"Thanks," I said, glad to be facing away from him so he couldn't see my perma-grin. I bit my lip so no one else would see it, either.

"How's everything?" he asked cryptically. I took it as him asking about Brandon but being careful since other sardines could be listening in.

"Seems, um, copacetic," I said.

"Cool beans."

The elevator stopped abruptly, causing me to lose my balance and fall against Joey's muscular chest. He put a hand on my hip to steady me, and it's a miracle I didn't die on the spot. He touched me all the time when we did "Summer Nights" together, but this was different.

"Sorry," I said quickly.

"No biggie," Joey said, shrugging and making his way out of the elevator.

Wes had taken the first car down and was waiting for me in his matching yellow poncho and borrowed flip-flops. They'd offered them to everyone as protection against the waterfall spray, but only a few of us had raised our hands.

"What's up?" he asked as we walked the tunnel toward the viewpoint. "Why do you have a clown smile?"

"My hair smells good."

Wes leaned over and sniffed. "Smells normal."

"Not according to Joey," I said excitedly. I grabbed his arm and whispered, "What if he likes me?"

We came to the end of the tunnel and stepped into daylight. Just before our conversation was swallowed up by the roar of rushing water, Wes asked, "What if?"

AFTER WE "ALMOST died" according to Wes on the appropriately named Hurricane Deck, which is a platform that they might have put just a little too close to the underside of the falls, I wanted to go to the gift shop and Wes wanted to find Tuesday, so we did our signature handshake, then squished away in opposite directions.

I rode the elevator alone, then pulled my wet mop into a ponytail, wrapping a scrunchie around it twice. I fished my Walkman out of my fanny pack, popping in the only mixtape I had with me: the *Pump Up Mix*.

I pressed play.

All along the winding, paved path to the gift shop, I stepped in time with the beat and mouthed the lyrics, my mouth slamming shut when anyone went by. First up on the playlist was "The Safety Dance" by Men Without Hats.

And we can act like we come
From out of this world

It was a mega challenge not to do the move from the video, where the singers arch their right arms over their heads and arch their left arms under their stomachs like weird broken scarecrows every other drumbeat—but I managed to just walk regardless.

The path was long enough for me to listen to "Holiday" by Madonna, "Cruel Summer" by Bananarama, and "Head Over Heels" by The Go-Go's. I felt totally pumped by the time I walked into the gift shop, like a girl who had things to look forward to: vacations and summers and romances with—

Joey! Joey was right there in the gift shop!

He didn't see me come in, so I ducked behind the spinning rack of postcards. I halfheartedly shopped while he and Shane cracked up trying to hit each other with Niagara Falls souvenir flyswatters. They both had wet hair from the Hurricane Deck. Joey looked like he could barely breathe, he was laughing so hard. It made me smile until Shane bumped into a stack of posters and made them wobble.

One of the shopkeepers said, "Young men, if you're not going to buy those, kindly put them back." She crossed her arms over her chest and waited.

Joey immediately dropped his flyswatter into the basket where it'd been and stepped away, looking sheepish. When Shane didn't react, Joey grabbed his friend's flyswatter and did the same.

"Take a chill pill," Shane said to the lady. I don't know if she heard him. "Let's motor, Joey, this place is stale."

They snaked their way around tables of sweatshirts and racks lined with key chains, Joey following Shane's lead, Shane muttering about how the shopkeeper was a heinous witch. I thought that was pretty extreme and expected Joey to say so, but instead he replied, "Totally, dude. And did you see those clothes?"

"You *know* she spends Saturday nights alone," Shane said, laughing.

Joey noticed me next to the postcards and stopped short.

"Oh, hey, Finnegan," he said, looking uncomfortable. "You're everywhere today. What are you, like, following me?" He laughed at his own joke, wringing his hands.

"I . . ." I didn't know what to say or even how to speak, so caught off guard by this different Joey. It made me default to self-conscious Stevie. I picked up a postcard. "I'm getting this for . . . my friend. You, um, don't know her."

I hoped he didn't ask this mystery friend's name.

"Did you see . . ." He gestured toward the flyswatters, then glanced at Shane, who was waiting by the door. "How long have you been here?"

"I just, um, like, right now," I lied. "See what?"

"Nothing."

"Cool."

"Cool."

I wanted to say something witty and make him turn back into the other Joey, which would then turn me back into more confident Stevie, but I was a floppy disk wiped clean.

"Dude, let's book," Shane said impatiently.

"Later, Finnegan," Joey said.

"La-bye."

Joey chuckled as he walked away, me rolling my eyes at myself for being unable to keep it together through a whole conversation with him. I lingered in the gift shop, slowly turning the postcard rack but not seeing any of the cards, wondering which Joey was the real Joey—the sweet one in mismatched socks or the kid who was rude to salespeople when no one else was looking.

10.

THE SECOND WEEK of the tour began in Boston, and during a free hour before the show, I made two important decisions. The first was to forget about how Joey had acted in Niagara Falls, and the second was to keep mailing the dedications.

As Wes and I walked the Back Bay neighborhood, gazing at the tightly packed brownstones built two hundred years ago, tripping over uneven cobblestones on streets only wide enough for horse-drawn carriages, Wes didn't know it, but he was helping me decide.

"You think I'm nice, right?" I asked.

"Except when you yell at me," he said.

"I never yell at you."

"You did that one time," he said.

"Okay, but generally, you think I'm nice?" He nodded. "Well, what if one day, I just seemed completely different, and I was rude to, like, an adult. And I laughed at you."

"I'd tell you to knock it off," Wes said. "Those old-fashioned lampposts are rad."

"Totally," I agreed. "But back to my question, would you automatically think I'm a mean person or just that I was having a bad day?"

"Duh. What's this really about?" He popped his gum.

"Nothing," I said. "Let's go to the right. I think I see a blue mailbox up ahead."

Backstage, everyone bubbled with energy because we were performing at a massive high school auditorium and the show was sold out. Plus, we'd been able to add in the coolest number, "Magic," since the venue wasn't carpeted like most of the churches we'd performed in so far and there was good ventilation.

"Magic" was a song from an awesome movie about roller-skating angels or witches or something called *Xanadu*—which is why it was performed on roller skates! Wes's sister Holly was in the number, as were Amy, Christy, and a fifteen-year-old named Wendy, who never talked to me.

When "Magic" was in the show, it had to be third to last

so the audience wouldn't be poisoned by the smoke machine. It probably would have been better if it was *actually* last, but Margo wanted to finish the show with two upbeat, full-cast numbers. That's why the venue had to be well ventilated, so Mr. Schneider and Mr. Johnson could throw open the windows or turn up the fans at the end of "Magic," and everyone would live long enough to put some money in the donation top hats.

The whole Boston performance was rad, but when it was finally time for "Magic," there was electricity in the air. The rest of the cast huddled together in the wings to watch.

Fog crept up the center aisle like it had a secret it would never ever tell—don't even ask—and the song began. I think Mr. Schneider majorly pumped up the volume, because that first note always startled me. Then it settled into a low, lazy beat that I could feel deep in my bones.

Nothing happened for the first four bars, and everyone waited in anticipation, even those of us who'd seen "Magic" happen a million times. Then, right before Olivia Newton-John started singing in her angelic (or witchy) voice, one at a time, the cast members appeared through the fog.

Holly floated in a fluttery light blue dress with one shoulder exposed. Her feathered auburn hair blew behind her as she skated down the aisle, always making eye contact with someone in the audience just as ONJ sang, with Holly lip-synching along to the lyrics . . .

Come take my hand

Right on her heels came Wendy in a lavender dress that tied at the neck, fake singing her part, then Amy in uncharacteristic pink and a silver-sequined headband, doing hers.

Christy was last, and sometimes people actually gasped when they saw her, she looked that much like Olivia Newton-John had in *Xanadu* in her blousy white dress that hung off both shoulders with the slit all the way up the right leg and the gold belt wrapped around her waist.

I loved watching Christy in "Magic," and not just because her roller-skating was the best or her costume was the raddest. Christy had a stage presence I wanted. Even though performing made me more confident in general, Christy was effortless—not like she never messed up, but like when she did, even the mess-up was mesmerizing.

Margo said we were all stars, even me, but I wanted to shine as brightly as Christy did, onstage—and off.

The girls on skates launched into an intricate roller dance, using every inch of space they had, zooming apart, then whizzing past one another, twirling before suddenly stopping in unison when the chorus went:

You have to believe we are magic

They lip-synched so well, it appeared that they were actually singing the song. At the same time, they swished their arms from side-to-side at their hips, gliding left, then right, with the music. Everything was perfectly in sync since they'd all performed together so long.

"I'd love to be in that number someday." Tuesday stood next to me in her costume for the finale numbers: a black sweatshirt with a shiny white satin star embroidered on the front and black pants.

I took a deep breath in the hopes it'd help my words come out like I meant them.

"Me too," I admitted, "but I can only make left turns on skates."

She giggled, scrunching into herself to keep quiet, then whispered, "It's easy to do a crossover. I can show you back at home!"

Tuesday's family owned the best skating rink in Cheyenne, called the Rock 'n' Roll. The place had photos of her all over the walls, posing with skating trophies that went way back to when she was just a toddler.

I imagined doing the couples' skate with Joey to "The Search Is Over" and got butterflies.

This was the second time that Tuesday had made an offer to hang out—I wondered if I'd been wrong when I'd assumed she was just being nice. I wondered if Tuesday was different from Jennifer T., if Tuesday would actually follow through with her invitation.

I thought of my mom telling me that everything was easy with friends after you took the first step, that all you had to do was act interested. She'd read that in some book about winning friends.

"Okay," I said softly, accepting the offer, cautiously hoping it was real. I felt Wes watching us, ready to force me to repeat the entire conversation to him the second Tuesday was gone.

Wes had helped me so much in my plan to tell Joey I liked him; I realized I'd hardly done anything to help him back.

"You know, Wes is a good skater," I whispered to Tuesday. "Maybe, um, like, when you, like, show me . . . you know, um, how to turn, Wes could come and, like, help out and . . . uh . . . we could get Slurpees. Or something."

"Of course, Wes is so sweet!" Tuesday said over the applause when "Magic" ended. I smiled, feeling good about accepting her offer and about helping Wes, knowing that he was going to lose his mind when I told him.

Tuesday was still talking. "When you learn how to turn right, you and me can try out for 'Magic' when Holly and Wendy leave Synchronicity!"

"Cool!" I said excitedly before mentally rewinding the tape player on what she'd said. "You mean when they go to college in two years? They're going into eleventh."

Margo walked onstage to stall while the "Magic" performers raced to the changing room to swap out dresses and skates for sweatshirts and black pants. Margo began the speech we probably all had memorized about how children need the arts like fish need water, and should be allowed to participate if they're interested, not just if they excel. She told the story of her daughter who stopped singing forever after being told she wasn't good enough for choir.

"No, don't you remember?" Tuesday said, back to whispering since Margo was talking. "Some kids are leaving after tour

because they're doing football and cheerleading and stuff. Practices and rehearsals conflict, so they had to pick."

"Oh," I said, feeling embarrassed for not knowing. "No one told me."

"How could you not know?" Tuesday whispered, looking at me, confusion written all over her elvish face.

"What do you mean?"

She shrugged. "I just figured you'd know since your brother's one of them. He made it."

"The *cheerleading* squad?" I asked, totally confused.

Tuesday laughed quietly. "You're so funny! No . . . football, *duh*. I mean, look at how big he's gotten. He'll be awesome at it!"

"But he's, um . . . he's never played on the team before," I whispered, eyeing Brandon, who was listening attentively to Margo's speech, his hands clasped in front of him.

"That's cool he's going to try something new!" Tuesday said. "I know a girl who went out fo—"

I stopped paying attention to Tuesday because I was freaking out. Brandon, my brother with a serious medical condition, was going to play *tackle* football? Was that even possible? And why hadn't he mentioned any of this to me?

Brandon and I told each other everything, from fears to dreams to crushes. He'd known about Joey since the day after I fell out of the tree, and even though Brandon had once told me to "be careful," and another time kind of implied that Joey was a flirt—which is a total falsehood, duh—Brandon was nice and

didn't tease me about Joey. And Brandon told me stuff about his love life, too. I knew there was some girl named Janice that he'd French-kissed behind the pool changing room but didn't like anymore, and that another girl named Mandy had asked him if she could write him on tour, but he'd said no since he didn't know where to tell her to mail the letters.

Why didn't I know this?

As if he'd heard my thoughts, Brandon suddenly looked at me. I held up my hand, HELLO. He held up his hand: HELLO back.

I'm worried about you, I thought at him.

He looked away.

The "Magic" girls returned.

It was time to say good night to Boston.

11.

WEDNESDAY MORNING, AS we drove into the Big Apple, the skyscrapers stood on tiptoe, reaching toward the sun, clustered together like best friends. I was awestruck.

"I think our big-city apartment with your betta fish should be here," I said to Wes. We were in the middle row of the Johnsons' minivan, and Mr. Johnson was swearing up a storm.

"You haven't even seen the city yet," Wes said.

"But look!" I gestured toward the steel, glass, and brick ahead of us. "And look," I said, pointing at the beat-up yellow cabs weaving in and out of lanes next to us, nearly hitting us, causing Mrs. Johnson to say, "Oh lord!" over and over again. "It's already better than anything we've ever seen."

"New York City is the most awesome place there is," Tuesday said, flipping around in her seat. "My mom brought me once for a skate competition, and do you even *know* how many shows they have on Broadway?"

"How many?" Wes asked, dropping his precious *Dragon* magazine on the floor and not even seeming to care.

"I don't know, like, a ton," Tuesday said, laughing.

"We're moving here," Wes boasted.

"Great! I'll come with you!" Tuesday said.

"We're getting a betta fish named Reginald!" Wes said, and I shook my head because that was such a weird thing to say—but Tuesday didn't think so.

"My grandpa's name is Reginald," she said sweetly. "And I have a betta fish at home. Her name's Lady."

Then Mrs. Johnson told her to "sit right," so she turned around.

"I'm dead," Wes whispered, staring blankly at the brown leather seat.

"I know, buddy," I said, patting his hand and laughing quietly, thinking Wes and Tuesday really were perfect for each other, hoping that one day, when he finally told her how he felt, she would say she felt the same way.

THE CHAPERONES DROPPED us in Central Park. They told us the older kids were in charge and abandoned us to find parking

places for the caravan. I guess you couldn't just parallel park a Winnebago in New York City.

The kids who'd been in the Winnie looked shell-shocked after riding through the congested streets.

"I thought Margo's head was going to explode," I overheard someone say.

"She got honked at so many times!" someone else said, laughing loudly. "I thought that last cab was going to ram us on purpose."

"Would you have blamed him?"

"Sounds like your mom doesn't like driving in New York," I joked to Wes.

"Glad we weren't in the Winnie," he said.

The plan was to take the subway to the bottom of Manhattan and walk back up. The chaperones would meet us eventually at Radio City Music Hall.

We came out of Central Park at the weirdest intersection ever, with cars and cabs zooming in a circle, heading toward or away from the park. My mouth hanging open, my eyes crawled up a nearby building, floor by floor. I wondered how many people were inside.

"It's incredible," I said to myself, wiping the sweat from my forehead. "Look at all of . . . this." I waved my hand around at fluffy trees and people who didn't look like me and architecture and cyclists and ONE WAY signs and water towers on rooftops and *everything*.

I could smell exhaust, hot garbage, hot dogs, spices, melted

cheese, baking bread, perfume, mint gum, and a bunch of other things I couldn't place all at the same time. It was radical!

Heading down the steps to the subway, I added urine to my list of smells, but I didn't mind—we were boarding a New York City subway! When the train screeched to a stop and the doors slammed open, I hurried on, anxious about getting crushed when they closed, gripping the first pole I saw with both hands. Wes was across from me.

"Can we buy I LOVE NEW YORK T-shirts and still wear them when we live here with Tuesday and Reginald?" he asked.

"How could we *not* do that?"

I looked over at Brandon, who was messing around with Josh, and Joey, who was comparing flexed muscles with Shane. Both Joey and Brandon confused me for different reasons: Brandon because he was keeping secrets, and Joey because I thought he might have been interested, or maybe be at least open to being interested someday, and then he was weird, and now I didn't know what was up.

"Everything okay?" Wes asked, reading my face.

I looked back at my friend and smiled. "Let's have the best day ever in New York, okay? Just us, no talk of crushes or . . . whatever else. Let's just have fun."

"I think I can handle that," he said, looking a little confused but like he was okay with it if that's what I needed.

Fifteen stops and only one head-bonk on the subway pole later, we reemerged aboveground. Twenty-six kids from

Wyoming who'd never been to the Big Apple before started walking north like a gargantuan gaggle of confused, sidewalk-blocking dorks. From the Financial District to Tribeca to Chinatown to Greenwich Village, I took it all in, excitedly pointing out sights to Wes and making him take pictures of me in front of fountains, on cobblestoned streets, and next to a parked taxi I pretended to hail.

We ate hot dogs and pizza and bagels, and even though one of the older girls kept reminding us to keep our hands on our purses and our eyes open, I wasn't afraid of New York; I was electrified by it.

The chaperones were smoking and laughing on the sidewalk outside of Radio City Music Hall when we finally made it late in the afternoon, greasy and sweaty like we'd showered in dirty water with our clothes on.

"It's about time!" said Margo.

"We were starting to get worried," Mrs. Johnson said.

"We walked, like, five thousand blocks," complained Kris.

"It wasn't *that* far," said Amy, rolling her eyes.

"My dogs are barking," said Little Josh, out of breath and sweating a ton. "But it was worth it."

"Totally," tons of kids echoed before launching into stories about things they'd seen or done on the way, and suddenly the adults were pummeled by chatter, trying to follow what we were saying, laughing through it all.

Finally, Margo clapped her hands together and told us to

follow her inside for a quick tour of the place where the Rockettes performed. We didn't actually *see* the Rockettes or get to watch them perform, but we did get free souvenir umbrellas and tote bags—which gave Wes the best idea ever.

"We need money for our New York apartment, right?" he asked. I nodded enthusiastically. "I have a business idea. Follow my lead and you'll get half."

"Okay," I said, not sure what he was up to but happy to play along.

Back on the sidewalk in front of Radio City Music Hall, it felt hotter than when we'd gone in even though it was around dinnertime. My hand immediately started to sweat holding the handle of the umbrella.

"How far do we have to walk to the hotel, Mom?" Wes asked Margo loudly.

"About ten blocks, give or take," Margo said. Several kids narrowed their eyes; we all knew that when Margo said "give or take," it really meant she had no idea. The hotel could be across the street or back in Connecticut for all we knew.

Wes cleared his throat. "If you don't want to carry your umbrella or tote bag, we will." He gestured between us. "For a dollar per person."

"Aw man, that's a rip-off!" Shane said while Tuesday immediately shoved her way through the crowd, umbrella and tote bag dangling from her outstretched hand, digging in her purse with the other.

"Thank you so much, guys," she said, handing over the items and her dollar before exaggeratedly fanning herself. "Best dollar I ever spent in my life."

Amy was next, then almost all the girls and at least half of the boys went for the deal. Wes and I slung piles of tote bags from our shoulders and draped umbrellas from our arms, the wooden handles digging into our skin.

We looked like junior traveling salespeople, and Wes and I couldn't help but laugh at each other as we tried to navigate the streets without hitting anyone with an umbrella or dropping our entire armloads in one of the smelly puddles that somehow existed despite the rainless day. It was a great distraction from worrying about Joey or Brandon, and a funny story to take home, so the pain and effort were worth it.

What made it even more radical was that Margo had overestimated the distance to the hotel. This time, her "give or take" worked in our favor.

In five blocks, each eight dollars richer, we were there.

12.

"STEVIE, GO GET some ice, will ya?" Robyn Rose asked, waving me away like she was an adult. "My RC is hot."

Robyn looked at Wendy like she was telling her something through telepathy.

"Yeah, mine too," Wendy said quickly, holding up what I guessed was an empty soda can. Those were the first words she'd said to me all tour—I'd kind of forgotten what her voice sounded like.

"Pretty please," Holly said, batting her eyelashes at me. With auburn hair and hazel eyes like Margo's, curves, and a great big smile, Holly didn't look a thing like her twin sister, Kris—or like

Wes. She looked like their oldest sister, though, the one who'd aged out of the group and didn't tour anymore.

The older girls may have been asking me to get ice, but what they really meant was, *Get lost.*

Robyn, Wendy, and Holly were all around the same age, about to start tenth or eleventh grade, and Robyn had been telling a story about going out with some guy she likes. But when she'd gotten to a part about how they'd driven out north of town, just the two of them, suddenly, she'd become desperate for ice.

"It's not like I've never heard of kids making out before," I muttered to myself, forcefully swinging the empty bucket as I wandered down the hotel hallway. "It's not like I'm *nine*."

I felt nine, though. I felt younger than nine, being banished like that.

I wished I could figure out where Wes was in this big, huge building, and we could go to the lobby and play Uno or something, but I had no way of contacting him. I decided to take the elevator to the top floor and work my way down the halls, thinking maybe Wes would magically appear.

Instead, after my third elevator ride, I turned a corner and ran smack into Joey.

Two empty ice buckets clattered to the ground.

"Sorry," I muttered, reaching down for mine.

"No prob," Joey said, chasing his, which had rolled across the hallway. "Looks like we're headed the same way." He held up

his empty bucket before looking left, then right, then toward the elevator bank. "Are you on this floor?"

I shook my head, thinking he sounded more like mismatched-socks Joey than flyswatter Joey.

"No ice machine on yours?"

I shook my head again, turning pink, hoping he wouldn't go on a truth-finding mission to prove me wrong. *Aha! You traveled eight floors out of your way! Explain yourself!*

Joey was barefoot, in gym shorts and a baggy white T-shirt, his dark hair a little mussed up, still fine as usual. He started down the hallway to the left, looking over his shoulder at me. "You coming, Finnegan?"

"Oh yeah, right, yeah."

I trailed behind Joey, glad I was still in my cute aqua romper and moccasins, not my Pegasus pajamas . . . again. I touched the end of my wavy hair; it'd grown an inch since we'd left thanks to frequent shampooing and was now well below my collarbone. Thankfully, I was no longer a fuzzy bowling ball.

I cleared my throat.

Joey looked back again, his deep, dark eyes giving me a jolt.

I didn't say anything.

He faced forward.

I could have kicked myself.

We walked by a mirror and Joey checked his reflection, running his free hand through his hair. *I* wanted to run my fingers through his shampoo-commercial hair!

We made it to the ice closet, and Joey lifted up the stainless-steel lid, exposing piles of perfect cubes for the taking. Even though the lid could stay up on its own, Joey held on to the top.

"Ladies first."

He was *definitely* mismatched-socks Joey.

I'd never been self-conscious about dragging a plastic bucket through ice before, but there's a first time for everything.

I stepped away quickly so he could take his turn, willing myself to say something, anything, and not miss this chance. I could practically hear Wes screaming at me, but nothing came to mind. Thankfully, Joey didn't have that problem.

"I know I can't tell anyone, and I won't, I swear, but, like, dude, your brother . . ." He sighed. "It's, like, stressing me out."

Maybe it was because it was a topic I knew well, or because it wasn't about me, or Joey, or us, but I spoke without sputters. "I get it. The first time Brandon had a seizure, we were home alone, watching TV in the family room."

"No way."

"I thought he was kidding at first," I said quietly. He nodded, looking interested, so I continued. "Brandon's always trying to, like, crack me up, and I was thinking it was some weird joke, but then it didn't stop, and he was making that sound . . ."

"Like the other night."

"Totally. I was so afraid. I thought he was going to die."

"What'd you do?" Joey grabbed a piece of ice from his bucket and popped it in his mouth like popcorn, crunching it

as he listened. Having his attention focused entirely on me, me being able to have a real conversation with him—it felt like stepping outside on the first day of spring.

"I ran to the kitchen and dialed nine-one-one, and the operator told me to push Brandon onto his side, so I dropped the phone to the floor and ran back and did that, and pretty soon the shaking stopped, and then the ambulance came right as my parents were coming back from bridge club."

"I bet they were so freaked to find an ambulance in their driveway!"

"My mom totally lost it; she had no idea what'd happened. My dad's, like, more, you know, reserved. He just got in the ambulance with Brandon and left."

"Sounds like my grandpa," Joey said. He lived with his grandparents, but I didn't know why or feel like it was my place to ask.

The more we talked, the more comfortable I felt. It wasn't like talking to Wes, where I didn't think about it at all, but it was still okay. Wes knew about Brandon's epilepsy, but I hadn't told him about the seizure the other night, maybe because I'd wanted to keep the secret between me and Joey, however weird that was.

But I thought that Wes would be proud that I was speaking in full sentences and managing not to shout random alien names—and I was glad that the Joey from the flyswatter incident was long gone.

I grabbed some ice and crunched it, too, loudly over the persistent buzz of the machine, the full bucket cool against my hip.

"My dad told us later it'd been a seizure, but they didn't know why it'd happened," I said. "A year later, he had another one, but it was much smaller. We were at the pool and he just, like . . . spaced out, ya know? He didn't shake or anything that time."

"That still sucks—big-time," Joey said like he meant it.

"It does. But now he takes medicine, and it makes the seizures super rare. Except . . . you know . . ."

"Yeah."

We both crunched more ice; I was curious about something. Tilting my head, I asked, "Have you heard about Brandon making the football team?"

"He'd be allowed to do that?" Joey said, surprised.

I shrugged.

"I mean, I guess if a doctor says it's okay . . ."

"That's the thing, though, I don't know if Brandon's told our parents, so how would a doctor even, like, know about it?"

Joey scratched his chin. "Well, where'd you hear it from?"

"Tuesday. And I was like, no way! I just don't get why Brandon wouldn't tell me."

Joey laughed a little. "Ah, that's nothing; I don't tell my sister anything."

"You have a sister?" I asked, scrunching up my forehead, focusing on this new information instead of trying to defend my super-good relationship with my brother and the fact that he really did tell me most stuff. At least I thought so.

"If you call a four-foot-nine jerk who steals my tapes a sister, then yeah, I've got one of those," he said. "Got a little brother, too."

My mind was blown. "What are their names?"

"DeLeon!" someone yelled from down the hall. "What's taking so long with the ice?"

"Was that Courtney?" Courtney had the highest bangs in the cast and was totally pretty.

"Ah, yeah, we're all watching MTV," he said, nodding.

In my head, I commanded, *Invite me to come to your room and watch MTV!* I desperately wanted to be included.

But Joey just looked at his bucket and frowned. "It's starting to melt." Then he shrugged. "If they want unmelted ice, they can get off their lazy butts and get it themselves. Catch ya later, Finnegan."

And with that, Joey was gone.

13.

I'D HEARD ABOUT tour theme songs for years. Before we could tour ourselves, Wes and I would beg older kids to tell us the stories about the songs and why they were selected.

One tour's theme song was "Dancing Queen" by ABBA—the Spanish version, because a host family in Southern California played it for some cast members and they went bonkers over it.

Another year it was "Go Your Own Way" by Fleetwood Mac, because one of the chaperones kept making wrong turns and steering the caravan off course, and they had to cancel three performances because of it. That chaperone wasn't asked to return the following summer.

Two years ago, the theme song was "Heroes" by David Bowie. A few of the boys on that tour swore they'd seen David Bowie himself at a record store in Austin, Texas, and it'd set off a three-day cast-wide argument about the all-time best David Bowie song. "Heroes" won and was thus named the song of the tour.

I'd forgotten about the tradition until the night we performed in New York City.

The performance happened in an actual off-Broadway theater, with SYNCHRONICITY "A NIGHT AT THE MOVIES" on the marquee out front. One show had ended a run last Sunday, and another would begin in September, so we were there in a sweet spot when the theater was unoccupied. Somehow Margo had managed to get us in.

"I feel like a real star," I told Wes, standing front and center on the elevated stage, gazing out at the rows and rows of plush maroon chairs rising from the closed orchestra pit, another set in the balcony overhead. "Someone said this was one of the smallest theaters, but it looks gigantic to me."

"I wonder if anyone will show up," he said, sniffing and shifting.

I shrugged. "I don't care; it's rad enough just to perform on this stage."

Before Wes could say anything else, Ms. Freeman yelled at us to get a move on, so we quit gawking and started helping. I

turned around to find a place for the microphone stand I was holding. At the back of the stage, four of the oldest kids were sliding together the pieces of the wooden cityscape that served as our backdrop, made to look like skyscrapers at night.

A muscled, stressed-looking man I didn't recognize rushed out from stage left. He tipped forward as he hustled, like he might tip all the way over soon. He stopped right in front of me.

"Who am I talking to about the lights?" he asked, holding a clipboard, the other hand on his hip.

"Mr. Schneider?" I asked quietly.

"What's he look like?"

"A surfer math teacher?"

"Where's this Mr. Schneider?" the guy asked impatiently in a thick New York accent, wiping his brow with his wrist.

"Outside with the trailer . . . I think," I said, glancing around. Everyone was busy setting up, and all of the adults had disappeared.

"What's your name, kid?"

"Stevie?"

"Nice to meet you, Stevie, I'm Michael." He shook my hand like we were business partners, his firm grip large and calloused. "Listen, Stevie, we're tight on time and Mr. Schneider's not around, maybe he's gone surfing, so how's about you help me out here?"

"Okay," I said quietly. "Or we could find someone . . ."

"I trust you, Stevie," the man said. "I think you got this." He stepped toward me and tilted his clipboard in my direction. "I got the list with the spots by song, we're copacetic there, all good." He tapped his pen on the checklist. "But I need to know if you want the white or the blue floods at the beginning, and now that I see what you're working with here"—he gestured toward the nighttime cityscape—"you might want the star gobo." I noticed that his eyes were two different colors: one brown and one lighter, not blue but not green. An unidentifiable color. "So which is it, white or blue floods at the beginning?"

"Uh . . ."

"My personal opinion is blue adds more star quality."

"Okay, blue, then."

"Good choice." Michael made a note, then looked at me again. "Star gobo?"

"Um, yeah, I don't . . . remind me . . . I forget what a gobo is," I stammered. As if I'd ever heard the word *gobo* in my life.

"It's a screen with cutout shapes," he said quickly. "It goes in front of the light and projects the shapes." He gestured toward the back of the stage again, then said, "I could make the background look like the starry night sky. You want?"

Picturing it made me smile. "Yes!"

"Good choice," Michael said. "You've been very helpful, Stevie, thanks. Will you stay onstage while I rig it up, and we can make sure it looks right?"

"For sure!" I said, excited to see what I'd just approved.

"Okay, sit tight, Stevie," Michael said, heading back from where he'd come.

I helped Christy and Holly set up the star boxes, staggering them across the stage in alternating heights, how they'd need to be for our first number, "Summer Nights." Most of the adults came back, and it seemed like almost everyone was onstage when suddenly a voice boomed through the theater.

"Yo, Stevie, wave up at me so I know you can hear this."

Cast members stopped what they were doing and looked at me curiously. "Is that the voice of god?" Little Josh joked, making a bunch of people laugh, including Joey.

"It's Michael," I said quietly, my face burning. I waved weakly at Michael's silhouette, which was backlit in a booth beyond the last row of seats. He gave me a thumbs-up. "He . . ." I pointed up. "He's the light guy."

"Why's he talking to *you*?" Wendy asked. I preferred the first week of the tour when she hadn't said a word to me. This second week, we'd been assigned to the same car and the same hotel room last night, and I was realizing that she was just kind of a jerk. Plus, she snored.

"I helped him," I said so quietly I was basically talking to myself.

"Okay, Stevie, let's test out the lighting you picked!" Michael said.

"*You* picked the show lighting?" Wendy said. "Why is a *thirteen*-year-old making the lighting choices? Ohmigod. Mr. Schneider!"

Technically, I wasn't thirteen yet—I wouldn't be until the day before school started. Margo had made an exception for me, but I wasn't about to point that out to Wendy.

"Can it, Wendy." I heard my brother say.

"Yeah, dang, Wendy, rude much?" I heard *her* brother, Russell, stick up for me, too.

"Stevie has great ideas!" Christy said enthusiastically—which was just her being overly nice because when had I ever suggested an idea, great or otherwise, to Christy Hutchinson?

"I'm sure it's chill," Mr. Schneider said in his faux surfer voice. I didn't look at him or anyone else; I was frozen, wanting to crawl inside the star box next to me and hide.

"Okay, let me just see here . . . Oh, wait! You kids like music?" Michael asked, and a bunch of the cast shouted, "Yeah!" or "Totally!" up at him. "How's about we crank some tunes for Stevie's big reveal?" People hooted and clapped. "Okay, just a minute!"

Forget the star box—I wanted to run all the way back to Wyoming.

"How'd you get yourself into this one?" Wes asked, appearing out of nowhere right next to me. "I left you for, like, five and a half seconds."

"He just asked me some questions, and now . . ." I sighed. "Is Joey paying attention?"

"*Everyone's* paying attention. Joey . . . Tuesday, who I might have mentioned is the coolest girl in the entire world."

I snorted with laughter and brushed my hair off my shoulder, feeling better just having Wes right next to me.

"Okay, I've got it now," Michael said. "Here's a new one for your collections, kiddies."

A song I'd never heard began blasting through the theater sound system. There wasn't much of an intro: The lyrics started right away, several voices singing at once.

We built this city

Pause.

We built this city on rock and roll

"I love this one!" someone shouted.

"Me too!" a few older kids agreed.

A catchy pop beat began, and my shoulders couldn't help but to bounce along with it. A man sang something about not recognizing people and hoopla and macaroni—it didn't make sense—but I liked the song anyway. It was about building a city while we were literally building our city onstage.

Michael said, "Okay, here it comes!"

The chorus played, and at the part when the male and female singers belted out *rock and rooooooll*, Michael switched off the lights, and everyone gasped.

The stage was a dream.

The light and dark colors popped, and the rest was tinted a shade of blue that seemed more mischievous than melancholy. At the back of the stage, beyond the wooden skyline, was Michael's night sky projected on a massive backdrop, dozens of tiny stars everywhere.

Christy looked at me, beaming. "Wow!"

"It's rad, Steves," Brandon called over the music.

"Maybe you should do the lighting all the time," Wes said.

"No way," I said. "But thanks."

Joey gave me a double thumbs-up just as Michael cranked it up even louder. No one could hear one another anymore, so we just listened. Michael had no idea, but he'd given us our tour theme song.

A few kids started dancing, and others joined in. Christy did sign language along to the chorus. She stacked her hands higher and higher to sign BUILT.

She tapped her fingertips together like little rooftops for CITY.

I mimicked her motions, proud of myself for making decisions that everyone seemed to like.

Tuesday waved me and Wes over to dance with her and Amy, and Wes sprinted across the stage to join them. Happy that Wes was getting a moment with his dream girl, I could have easily shied away into the shadows. But I danced over, proud of myself for that, too.

I spun around and landed facing Joey. Smiling warmly, he mouthed, "Good job."

I didn't turn into a tomato.

I didn't look away.

I lifted my chin, smiled back, and mouthed, "Thanks."

14.

THURSDAY, AUGUST 8, 1985

Dear Mr. Kasem,

Hi! My name is Stevie Finnegan, and I'd like to make a Long-Distance Dedication to a boy named Joey. We're touring in a performing group, and I want to tell him how I feel about him, which is that I like him a lot more than as a friend.

I hope you will play "Crazy for You" by Madonna for Joey. There was this thing that happened earlier tonight before our performance when he, like, just looked at me onstage, and it felt meaningful, you know?

This part of the song gives me chills: "I see you through the smoky air. Can't you feel the weight of my stare?" I also really like it when Madonna sings about how when they're looking at each other they don't need words. I don't always say things the way I'm thinking them, so I can relate to that.

Sincerely,
Stevie Finnegan

PS: Sorry my handwriting is sloppy. I'm writing in the dark because one of the girls I'm staying with yelled at me for having the lamp on.

15.

WE'D CLOSE OUT week two with three performances in Washington, DC.

Friday evening, we arrived at the Gallaudet University campus. Gallaudet is a college for deaf and hard of hearing students—Christy's mom went there and got us the gig . . . and made it so we could stay in actual college dorms. The show was going to be especially rad because instead of performing like normal, Christy was going to interpret the whole thing.

Everyone lined up behind the trailer to take in sets and props and costumes without any of the chaperones having to tell us. Like a machine, Mr. Schneider and Mr. Johnson passed items to

kids in line, Mr. Schneider racing in and out of the trailer to get stuff and Mr. Johnson huffing and puffing as he handed it over. Robyn Rose ticked every item off on a clipboard.

"Hey, Christy, how do you sign, 'I think you're cute,' you know, like just in case I see a hot deaf dude?" I heard Holly ask behind me. I struggled to walk without dropping a heaping pile of black plastic costume bags, hangers peeking out the top, smacking me in the face every time I took a step.

"It's not like I can show you right now," Christy replied with a laugh. I glanced back at them; they each had hold of a side of one of the sets of nesting star boxes. "I'm kinda nervous to interpret. I don't want to, like, embarrass my mom or anything."

"As if!" Holly said. "Your mom thinks you're the greatest thing since sliced bread. Every time she comes to one of our shows, she smiles so big it looks like it hurts."

"She loves the whole group," Christy said. "She always laughs at the air guitar. She says it's like she can really hear it! That's why she wanted us to perform here."

"That's totally sweet," Holly said, and I grinned like I was part of the conversation—until the toe of my shoe caught a raised sidewalk seam and I nearly went down like a sack of potatoes.

Christy and Holly both laughed. It sounded friendly, not mean, but my neck still turned red.

We arrived at the imposing two-story brick auditorium. Seven massive pillars held up the flat roof. The center double

doors were propped open for us; inside, a pair of double doors to the auditorium were held open, too.

"We Built This City" was blasting from Little Josh's boom box.

My stomach flipped as I started down the center aisle toward the stage: There were a lot of seats. After I made my way to the front and dropped my costume bags in a pile with a bunch of others to be organized, I turned and saw that above the main floor was a balcony with even more rows of seats.

Those could hold a lot of people.

Half the cast was busy onstage, setting things up, yelling over the song and one another about what went where. Several of the boys, including Joey, were assembling the cityscape sets, making sure they were lined up so the middle building wasn't cut in half. Joey's black hair was especially shiny under the stage lights: It was like he had a halo around him. I was a crushed grape in a field of—

"Take a picture and it'll last longer." I flipped around to find my brother smirking next to me.

"Shut up!" I said, smacking him, my cheeks blazing. Thankfully, right then, Little Josh was badly singing, "On rock and rooooooll," at the top of his lungs, so I didn't think anyone had heard Brandon.

I stepped closer to him.

"Hey, Bran, we haven't really talked since—"

"Gotta run," he interrupted. "Amy said her mom wants me in the dressing room. Something about ripped pants."

"Okay," I said, wondering when, and why, Brandon had decided to avoid me. But I didn't have much time to dwell, because I was rushed backstage for makeup.

The audience would arrive soon.

I PEEKED OUT from backstage while Margo gave her opening speech, with Christy interpreting beside her.

I was spellbound watching Christy sign and wondered if she'd learned English or sign language first. I wished I was such good friends with her that if someone asked, I could be like *of course* she learned to sign first, *duh* person-who-doesn't-know-Christy-like-I-do.

I got a start when I happened to check on Joey and found him already looking at me. He pointed at my hair and did a thumbs-up. Tuesday and Amy had styled it before the show. Like a duo of professional hairdressers, they'd flat-ironed away the perm, then crimped my hair into perfect crinkles and pulled it up into a high side ponytail, my bangs swept to the side and crimped, too. It looked wicked!

When Margo saw it, she said it didn't go with my costume for "Summer Nights," but she let me keep it like that anyway after Tuesday pointed out that no girls in the fifties had rad

side-shaved hair or four ear piercings like her, either.

From the first beats of "Summer Nights," the people in the audience beamed at us, and that made performing even more fun. Shane's older brother, Trevor, and Holly stepped up for their solos, and the rest of us lip-synched backup, and I felt like I would never *stop* smiling.

Joey and I faced each other and clasped hands at exactly the right moment before the dance part, my hands feeling tiny in his larger ones, both of us performing our best, the act of being perfectly in sync with Joey firing me up even more.

It didn't hurt that he looked completely fine in his leather jacket with the collar popped, his dark hair slicked back on the sides.

And at the end, after the entire cast slowly raised our open palms toward the ceiling in time for the dramatic last note, the audience erupted into applause and stood up like it was the end of the show, not just the beginning.

Holding the final pose for five counts like Margo always told us to do, I couldn't help but giggle. Holly, in front of everyone else, frozen in her dance dip, supported by Trevor, had the most genuinely gleeful smile plastered on her face. Wes looked like he might explode from happiness. Everyone did.

"This is so rad," Tuesday said from the medium star box next to me, applause washing over us. "They're the best audience we've ever had!"

"For sure," I said, insides warm, full of pride. "I can't wait for the rest! It's going to be the best show ever!"

The spotlight turned off, our cue to make like a tree and leave if we weren't in the next number, "9 to 5." Kids helping turn the stage into a pretend office rushed around. As I went by Christy on my way toward the wing, I touched her arm.

"Hey, good job interpreting," I said.

She looked surprised, maybe because I wasn't usually the one to speak first, or maybe because she didn't get a lot of random compliments about her signing. "Thanks, Stevie!"

"Not that I know what you're saying," I added quickly.

"I could show you some signs sometime," she said. "It's pretty awesome and then you could talk to my parents."

"Totally!" I whispered.

"Christy," Robyn Rose whispered, "we're taking our places."

"Thanks again," Christy said, blond hair in a high ponytail, bright blue eyes sparkling even in the dark. She stepped forward, leaned down, and gave me a quick-but-firm hug before I had time to think about it. She went to stage right and I rushed backstage, thinking about how even though Brandon was awesome, I wouldn't mind having an older sister like Christy, too.

I watched all of "9 to 5," and it was rad as usual: Holly, Robyn, and Courtney totally killed it. At the end, the audience cheered even louder, and many of them waved their hands in a twisting motion. I didn't know what it meant, but it seemed positive, and the energy of the show built from there.

"Ghostbusters" was extra hilarious.

The choreography in "It's the Hard Knock Life" was extra precise.

"Magic" was extra special.

And when we did the two finale songs back-to-back, "So Long, Farewell" from *The Sound of Music* and "Don't You (Forget About Me)" from *The Breakfast Club*, with the entire cast performing at one hundred percent, Courtney even nailing the roundoff-back-handspring she never wanted to do, I wished the night would go on forever. I was glad to be spending the last month of my summer doing something probably no other twelve-almost-thirteen-year-old in the country was doing.

"Don't You (Forget About Me)" got to the part that says, "la, la, la, la," which was fun to dance to, and Mr. Schneider lowered the lights, the white satin stars on our black sweatshirts beginning to glow, me glowing, too.

The cast took off the black gloves covering white ones underneath, the black light making our hands shine in the darkness like actual stars, and the crowd went nuts. The applause seemed to last half an hour.

EVERYONE WAS ON top of the world after the show, spilling into the back hallway with energy like we'd had thirty Pixy Stix each. Kids ran into one another and the walls, smacking arms and

hugging, slapping backs and tripping over their feet now that their coordination was off duty for the night as we moved toward the dressing room.

"Ms. Freeman said she was watching our moves extra closely tonight and didn't see one mistake!" Robyn said loudly.

"I'm glad she wasn't looking at me during 'Footloose,' then," Russell Gross joked, bashfully running a hand over his red mustache. "I tripped trying to do that new ball change thing at the Please Louise part.'"

"Please, Louise," two of the other boys sang in unison. Most of the rest of us joined in for the next line, and it was horrible—and hilarious! "Pull me off of my knees!"

"Wow!" Courtney said, her bangs bouncing. "That made my ears sad!"

Everyone busted up before resuming other conversations.

In the dressing room, each cast member found their pile of exploded costume bags and started cleaning up, searching for missing boxing gloves or socks, safety pins, or pancake makeup. People chugged sodas or water while they worked, dehydrated after the performance. As I was crossing to the left side of the room and Joey was crossing to the right, we got caught in a dance trying to get around each other.

I stepped right as he stepped left.

We both stepped in the other direction.

Then back to the first.

We lost it, Joey laughing at the ceiling like he did when he thought things were way funny.

"How about I freeze, and you move?" he asked.

"What if I wanted to be the one to freeze?" I asked, half smiling, not even realizing what I was saying or how flirty it sounded until it was already out of my mouth. I felt the warmth in my face that was sure to turn me into a tomato in seconds.

Joey smile-frowned. "Oh, really?"

That sounded flirty.

Was that flirty?

He took a step *toward* me, so close I could smell the RC on his breath.

I wanted to scream, OHMIGOD, JOEY DELEON IS FLIRTING WITH ME! but somehow managed to act normal . . . at least as normal as I was capable of acting.

"Yeah, really," I retorted, tipping my head a little.

"Well, all right, then, Finnegan," Joey said, dark eyes sparkling.

That seriously looks like flirting!

I didn't know what else to say, so I decided it was time to run away, but I couldn't budge until he went around me after making a big flirty deal about freezing.

"Go, then," I said, smirking at him like I'd won something. My face felt sunburnt.

"I'm going," he said with a laugh. But before he walked off, Joey twisted his lips, then said, "Something's different about you

lately." He squinted at me, adding, "The hair. It's rad."

It's a miracle my legs didn't give out right there.

"Thanks," I said quietly, sounding like shy Stevie, not whoever actively flirted with Joey five seconds ago. I cleared my throat. "I know it's rad!" I practically shouted at him, my cheeks as hot as an electric blanket.

Joey laughed and stepped around me. "Later, Finnegan."

16.

"THIS IS THE best month of my entire life," I said dreamily, replaying all the tour moments I'd had with Joey, from him keeping Brandon's secret to our hallway meetup in New York, to him watching me on the starry night stage, to our freeze dance earlier.

It really felt like . . .

"Okay for real I think Joey likes me!" I blurted out before covering my face in horror for having said it aloud. Wes and I were next to each other on my assigned bed at Gallaudet, backs against the concrete block wall, feet dangling.

"It's about time!" Wes said. "Now you can just go up to him tomorrow and tell him instead of us having to try to force him to listen to *American Top 40* again."

"No, I can't!" I said. "He has to hear it. That's the whole *thing*. Speaking of, I have to mail today's dedication."

"But it doesn't *have* to be the whole thing." Wes's stomach growled. Everyone was in their assigned spaces or milling around in the common room, waiting for pizza, soda, and cinnamon breadsticks after the performance of our lives. "You could just tell him and get on with your relationship."

"Says the kid who left a message on Tuesday's answering machine."

"Stop ragging on me," Wes snapped.

"What's *your* problem?"

He didn't say anything until I'd nudged him three separate times. Then, finally, he said, "You've just had all these *things* with Joey. I feel like a goober. I'm never going to get Tuesday to like me."

"You're not a goober, and yes, you will," I said. "Tuesday's always including you in things—like when we danced on the stage in New York. And she's going to move with us to our city apartment with Reginald, remember?"

"That's not *real*," he muttered. "She's just a nice person. Of course she is—she's an elf."

"Her saying she wanted to move with us to New York isn't real, even though it actually happened, but you referring to her as *elf* is?"

"You know I don't think she's a real elf," he snapped. "It's just the D&D character that makes the most sense for her. *God.*"

"Are we in one of those movies where the two main characters wish they could switch bodies and then it actually happens? Because you sound more like me than you. You're usually, like, more . . . optimistic."

"I'm starving to death," he groaned.

"Me too," I agreed, waggling my feet.

"Ugh," he groaned again, falling sideways into a pillow. "I'm dying of hunger and lovesickness."

"So you've said eight million times," I said. "Do you think Joey's in the common room?"

"How would I know?" Wes asked, his words muffled. "Not even my D&D character can see through walls."

As Wes started listing all the skills his character *did* have, I returned to my mental music video of me and Joey throughout the tour, deciding that yes, definitely, Joey DeLeon liked me back.

Suddenly I gasped, smacking my hand to my chest.

"What?" Wes asked, sitting up suddenly. "Is the pizza here?"

"What if he *does* like me back?"

"So, the pizza's not here?"

"Wes!" I exclaimed. "Stop talking about pizza! I'm serious!"

He sighed. "Fine. If Joey likes you, too, that's a *good* thing. That's what you want, right?"

I glanced at the open door and back at him, looking worried. "Yeah, of course."

"So then what's the problem? Isn't that the whole entire point of writing Casey Kasem five hundred letters?"

"Thirteen," I corrected. "One a day plus the day before we left."

"Isn't that the point of writing Casey Kasem thirteen billion letters—to get Joey to like you and go out with you?"

I rolled my eyes at his exaggeration but didn't get stuck on it because I had a real problem.

I leaned closer and whispered, "What if he wants to . . . like . . . you know?" I made meaningful bug eyes at Wes.

"What?" he asked.

"Come on."

"Seriously, what?"

I sighed loudly. "What if he wants to *kiss*? I've never kissed anyone!"

He didn't answer at first, then all in a rush, said, "Oh god, I haven't either—this is major."

"That's what I'm saying."

He scratched under the headband he'd put on after the show. "What if Tuesday wants to kiss when I finally tell her I like her?"

"That's what I'm saying!"

"She'd be good at it," he said, looking worried, his stomach growling loudly. "She's good at everything." He sighed like a grown-up when the bills come. "I'm not naturally good at anything."

"You're good at D&D."

He laughed. "That's not skill, it's strategy. It's different. I can't

think my way through kissing. In fact, I'm pretty sure thinking about it too much would actually make it worse."

"You're good at bike stunts," I offered.

"Don't you remember when I cheese-grated my face?"

"You're already thirteen—you're an official teenager, but I won't be until the end of the month."

"How is my age a skill?"

I was at a loss, and Wes stared at me, ready to challenge anything I said he was good at. Our eyes locked for so long it turned funny; he snorted, then I giggled, then he chuckled, and we both lost it.

After the laughtershocks died down, Wes said, matter-of-factly, "We need to practice kissing." I didn't answer at first. "We need to practice on each other," Wes clarified.

"What are you *talking* about?" I asked, looking at him like he was a human fart.

"I'm serious," he said, staring at me with an expression that did seem pretty darn serious.

"The only way I'm kissing you is if you turn into a pizza," I said, pushing him so hard he fell sideways again.

"I don't mean like *that*," he said, sitting up. "Not, like, kissing each other's *faces*—gag me. I mean just each other's . . . arms or something. So we can tell each other if it feels gross or okay or whatever."

"That is the worst idea you've ever had," I said, while simultaneously thinking maybe it wasn't the worst idea he'd ever had.

There was no one I trusted more than Wes to warn me that I kissed like a hungry leech and needed serious help.

Plus, it was possible my hunger had muted my ability to make good decisions.

"You first," I challenged Wes, offering him my forearm. I decided that if he did it, I'd do it. Plus, I was probably going to die of starvation before it was my turn anyway.

"I'm not kissing the hairy part," he said, grabbing my wrist and flipping it over roughly.

"My arm is not *hairy*," I said, snatching it back.

"Everyone has hair on their arms, dork," he said, pulling my arm back his way and gently turning it over again. His hands were clammy. "This is more . . . realistic."

"Okay, just do it already," I said, turning my face extra away from him and closing my eyes. I felt like I was going to pass out. "Get it over with!"

"Okay, okay!"

I heard him take a deep breath. I took a deep breath. And then I felt his lips pressed against my wrist, soft and warm, a little wet but not slobbery like my neighbor's basset hound. Wes kept his lips there for three seconds—I counted—then pulled away.

"So?" he asked, dropping my arm. "Was it . . ."

I covered my face, which was still turned away, eyes closed, to give my report. Through my hands, I said, "You're approved."

"Oh, thank god," Wes said, exhaling forcefully. "That was

stressful." I felt the bed bounce as he got comfortable, then he said, "Your turn."

Crap, I hadn't died yet.

I took my hands off my face, opened my eyes, and glanced briefly at my best friend, whose cheeks were as red as mine felt. Just as I was going to tell him *never mind*, he offered me his wrist, and I decided to go for it. He followed my unspoken rule of turning away and closing his eyes.

I picked up his forearm like it was corn on the cob and licked my lips, then dried them on my shoulder so they weren't too dry, but not soggy, either. Tiny tops spun in my hungry-hollowed insides as I leaned in, cologne filling my nostrils. I almost commented on that, but didn't, not wanting to mess with Wes when he was already freaking out about Tuesday.

I closed my eyes and pressed my lips to his slightly salty wrist, staying there for three seconds before pressing even firmer for one second and releasing Wes's corncob arm.

I smiled, knowing it hadn't been terrible even before I noticed that Wes's cheeks were redder than before.

"Also definitely approved," he said, smiling.

I opened my mouth to tell him—

"Um, like, what are you guys doing in here?" Amy asked, smirking from the doorway, book in one hand, soda in the other.

"Nothing," Wes said, jumping off the bed at total warp speed.

Amy laughed and went to put her book on her nightstand; we

were sharing the room. "Don't worry, I'm not a narc." She turned and faced us, Wes standing awkwardly in the middle of the room and me still back-to-the-wall on the bed. "Ready for pizza? It just got here."

Wes and I replied at the same time, "Let's go."

17.

SATURDAY MORNING, AFTER Kris agreed to fake earth-shattering cramps, making it so we couldn't leave to go sightseeing until after this week's Long-Distance Dedication aired over on the radio, the rest of us hung out in the Gallaudet dorm common room.

American Top 40 was cranked on Little Josh's boom box. Joey and some other kids played cards at one end of the dining table, and my brother, Tuesday, Josh, and Amy put a puzzle together at the other. Every couch, chair, and inch of beige carpeting was occupied by a sun-kissed, sleep-deprived kid. A bunch of us had sodas from the vending machine because there were no adults around to tell us not to.

Backs against the back of the couch, watching our crushes while trying not to be obvious about it, Wes and I messed around with my Magic 8 Ball. He held it out toward me. "Blow for luck."

I'd just asked if my most recent dedication would play today.

I leaned in, tossing my crimped hair over my shoulder, and blew like the ball was those birthday candles that refuse to go out. Wes shook hard and showed me the verdict: *Reply hazy, try again*

He shook it again. This time it said: *Cannot predict now*

I rolled my eyes and sighed right before Casey Kasem introduced the number twenty-one song on the countdown this week, "Raspberry Beret" by Prince.

"Tuesday would look great in a beret," Wes whispered when the chorus began. Then he looked at the Magic 8 Ball. "Does she like me?"

He shook the ball hard, read its response, and his eyes lit up.

Outlook good

We high-fived, and then I leaned my head on his shoulder for three songs, until he told me I was making his arm fall asleep. I was about to get up to take a pee break when, finally, Casey Kasem introduced the Long-Distance Dedication. I sat up straight. Wes elbowed me in the ribs, as if I wasn't already totally freaking out.

"This week's dedication goes out to . . ." Casey Kasem said.

"Does he look like he's listening?" I whispered, eyes on Joey as he threw a card onto a discard pile, making Shane groan loudly—which caused me to miss a chunk of what Casey Kasem said.

"Shane needs to clam up," Wes whispered back.

Casey Kasem continued. ". . . wanted to dedicate this love ballad to . . ."

Shane shouted, "You're such a cheater!"

"Oh my *god*!" I whispered harshly. "He's, like, totally ruining this!"

". . . because he's off serving our country in the army," Casey Kasem said, and I blew out my breath. It wasn't one of my dedications.

"Next week," I said, not so sure about that.

"Next week," Wes reassured me before standing up and offering his hand to pull me up, too. "Let's go tell Kris she can recover now."

18.

THE DAY AFTER my second failed attempt at telling Joey I liked him over the airwaves, we performed at a theater in a forest in Virginia that was like nothing I could have imagined. Facing out from center stage, I noticed that instead of connecting as two long sidewalls, the natural-wood wall panels were angled in, inviting fresh air and sunlight. There was no wall at the back of the theater, so I could see the bright green space beyond the seats and the blue sky above. And because the balcony was held by narrow beams that blended into the decor, it looked like it was floating in the sky.

"This place is wild," I said, awestruck.

"The guy said the original one burned down. He said it looked just like this, though." Wes liked to gather random facts. When he was bored at my house, he always read the encyclopedia.

"Huh, I bet that took a while. I think this is, like, the mega-hugest stage we've been on so far." I turned in a slow circle. "It's gargantuan."

"How long do you think it'd take to run across it?"

"Do it, I'll time you." It was universally known by us that Wes was faster than me.

After several tries, Wes and I determined that it took eight seconds to run across the stage—at least that's the best we could do before Ms. Freeman, wearing only purple, yelled at us to stop embarrassing ourselves.

Our selves hadn't been embarrassed, but we stopped anyway.

The event was a whole day of performances by a bunch of different types of entertainers, not just us, so instead of the full version of *A Night at the Movies*, we could only do three numbers.

"Today's lineup will be 'Eye of the Tiger,' 'Fame,' and 'Footloose,'" Margo announced in the dressing room, one foot ahead of the other, moving front to back like a human rocking chair as she spoke. "We Built This City" played low on the boom box in the background, and I was aware of Joey and Shane talking in hushed voices nearby, making each other snort-laugh, not paying attention to Margo, which I thought was kind of rude—and apparently Robyn did, too.

She flipped around and hissed, "Shh!"

"Someone's on her period," Shane muttered.

Margo didn't seem to notice any of it. "That combination presents . . ." she went on, looking down at the notebook paper in her hands, putting her index finger to her mouth. She nodded and continued her sentence. "The least amount of costume hassle, since the boys in 'Eye of the Tiger' just need to throw on T-shirts and sweatshirts for 'Fame.'" She looked around at a bunch of sunburnt faces. "It'll be fine."

"I'm in all three," Joey said, hooking his thumbs into the armholes of his muscle shirt and lacing his fingers together, showing off more of his shoulders. He looked adorable but sounded kind of cocky.

"I'm not in any," I murmured.

"Sucks to be you," Joey said, making Shane laugh, before strutting away like a rooster.

What the heck?

"Did you just see that?" I whispered to Wes.

"Huh?"

"Never mind."

Margo said that anyone not in the numbers should cheer loudly for their fellow castmates, then ran off to find Mr. Schneider, who we found out later was off flirting with a lady who worked at the theater. I hung around the dressing room for a while, then made my way backstage and stood near one of the

curtain pulley systems so I could watch the abbreviated show. I felt someone's presence next to me.

"Hello there," said a man with a thick accent. He had sand-colored hair, sunken eyes, and a warm smile. He wore a button-down shirt and vest on top and . . .

I looked away so fast I hurt my neck. His tights were *so* tight. And nude. And, like, practically see-through.

Ohmigod.

"Hello," I said, cheeks getting hot. He didn't seem to notice.

"You are part of this group?" he asked, gesturing toward the boys taking the stage for "Eye of the Tiger."

"Yes, I am," I said, forcing myself to look at him so he wouldn't think I was disrespectful. But I kept my eyes on his face, definitely not his bottom half. "You're a dancer?"

He laughed once, then nodded. "And you?"

"I'm a . . ." I screwed up my face, not knowing how to put it. Did he know what lip-synching was? And even though I danced, I wouldn't call myself a *dancer*. "I'm part of a show."

The Rocky theme song began, and the crowd out front started cheering. When the cast began to move, the man's stormy eyes lit up.

"Ah! I love this! You hop around and pretend you are singers!"

I felt silly until he held up a pretend microphone and started mouthing the lyrics to the chorus of "Eye of the Tiger." "Look at the people! You spread joy!"

I smiled and looked down at my shoes, thinking that, *Yeah, we do spread joy.* When people came to our shows, they went home happy.

The man was still lip-synching along when I looked back at him.

"Show me the moves!" he said. "This hopping dance, you know it?"

I laughed because yes, even though I was not in this number, I'd seen it performed so many times, I did know the steps.

"Okay, go like this," I said, putting up my dukes. He did it, too. "Punch the air, one, two, three, while you bob with your feet, like, yeah, you've got it. Then cross your foot over—your other foot—and turn around slowly when the guy holds the note, then jump your legs out like this when it says 'of the tiger.'"

"I got it," he said. "Let's do it again."

"Wait for the chorus," I said, adding quickly, "Here it comes." In unison, we lip-synched and performed the moves to the chorus together. Afterward, we beamed at each other, laughing quietly.

"I believe it is my turn next," he said after our three numbers were over. "Thank you for showing me your joy. I'll never forget it." He took a step away, then turned back. "What is your name, by the way?"

"Stevie," I said. "It's a nickname."

"And I am Misha," he said. "It's a nickname, too. It's a pleasure to meet you, Stevie."

"You too," I said, blushing. "Good luck with your dancing."

Misha nodded and shook my hand before he walked onstage. The crowd went completely bonkers; Misha smiled and waved, then got in position and waited, frozen. Classical music erupted from the orchestra pit.

Misha moved and my jaw dropped—he was so amazing at ballet I forgot he was practically bottom-half naked. I realized that it was good he was wearing tights because seeing his superhero-style leg muscles propel him high into the air was totally awesome and something I knew I'd never forget.

At the end of Misha's performance, the audience screaming for more, I noticed Margo across the stage in the opposite wing staring at me, her eyes huge like one of those lemurs at the zoo. She pointed in the direction of the dressing room; I thought I was in trouble for something, but I didn't know what.

I nodded, then made my way to the changing room. Once there, I sat down on the edge of a folding chair next to Wes and bit my fingernail.

"I think your mom's going to kill me," I reported.

"What'd you do?" Wes asked, poking his head through his T-shirt, which made his headband fall and momentarily cover his mouth.

"I have no idea," I admitted. "Talked to a stranger?"

Just then, Margo rushed through the door. "Everyone!" she shouted, making me jump. "Do you know what Stevie Finnegan just did?"

"Ohmigod," I whispered as the heat crept up my neck.

"Dude," Wes said. "You really are in—"

"She just talked to international ballet superstar Mikhail Baryshnikov!" Margo declared, and the room erupted into *ooh*s and *wow*s and *oh my god*s. Over everyone, Margo shouted louder, "Our own Stevie Finnegan just hung out with the best ballet dancer in the entire world!"

"He said his name was Misha," I said quietly. No one heard.

19.

MONDAY, AUGUST 12, 1985

Dear Mr. Kasem,

I'm Stevie Finnegan, and I'm writing to you from a Winnebago (which is so cool!) with a Long-Distance Dedication. This is like the fourteenth letter I've sent you, but I know a lot of people send letters and your mailbag is totally full, but I hope this one makes it on-air!

I'm traveling with a performing group, and so is the boy I like, Joey.

I listened to the song I want to dedicate last night,

and whoa, the lyrics really say what I want to say to Joey. To be honest, he's super-duper confusing. Like sometimes he seems like he totally likes me back, and other times he acts like he barely knows who I am. The part in the song when it says, "The love I'm sending ain't making it through to your heart" feels like <u>exactly</u> what's happening sometimes. And also, when she asks, "Don't you want someone to care about you?" It's like the whole entire song was written for me and Joey.

So, Casey, will you please play my Long-Distance Dedication of "What About Love?" by Heart for Joey?

Sincerely,

Stevie Finnegan

20.

I STARTED OFF the third week of our tour assigned to a host house in Charlotte, North Carolina, with just me and my idol Christy Hutchinson—which was rad and vom at the same time because it was like having a sleepover with the coolest girl in the world, and I didn't know if I was up for the challenge. I *did* secretly and in a silly way hope Christy would eventually let me adopt her as my new sister, so, riding home in the Robertsons' station wagon, I decided to see the host family assignment as an opportunity.

Mr. and Mrs. Robertson had two kids, a fourteen-year-old boy named Jason and a twelve-year-old girl named Jenny. Jason

and Jenny must have both been popular kids and done a lot of sleepovers, because they had beds to spare in their rooms: Jason had a bunk bed, and Jenny had two twins, both with trundles.

Besides worrying about embarrassing myself in front of Christy, I also worried about being left out because both Robertson parents and Jason were Deaf. Because of that, I didn't talk very much over dinner of sloppy joes and tater tots, leaving the chatter to Christy. Except I kept having to ask what was going on.

"What'd he say?"

"What'd she say?"

"Why's that light flashing?"

"What's so funny?"

I felt like an ignoramus, but Christy was patient.

"Mrs. Robertson just told a joke about a claustrophobic astronaut," she said, making the walls of a box in front of her, then making a sign that looked like two fives coming together, but not touching, toward her chest. After that, she crossed her pointer and middle fingers on her right hand and made it blast off, then put flat hands parallel to each other, palms facing, chopping once.

At least that's what it looked like to me; her hands moved pretty fast.

Christy speared a tater tot and popped it in her mouth.

"What's the punch line?" I asked.

Everyone else was still chuckling except Jenny, who had gone to answer the phone, which was why the light had been flashing.

I could see her through the doorway to the kitchen, spinning as she talked, the long phone cord twirling around her like a skinny mustard-yellow snake.

"He just needed a little space," Christy said and signed before she and the Robertsons cracked up again.

"Good one," I said, laughing and wishing I could tell the Robertsons my favorite joke, too.

The adults and Jason launched into a conversation in sign language, their hands moving in a blur. I heard slaps and thumps of hands hitting hands and chests, forceful exhales, soft grunts and groans. It was like how if you turned off the music at a school dance, you'd still hear the sneaker squeaks and sniffles. It wasn't silent, but it was quiet.

"Is this . . . like, um . . ."

Christy waited for me to spit it out.

"Like, um, does it sound . . . like this at your house?"

Was that a weird thing to ask? I didn't know, but I was curious about Christy's homelife. I was used to loud noises in my house—Brandon and his friends shouting while they played Atari or basketball outside, my mom yelling into the phone so my grandma could hear, the neighbor's dog barking through the fence, that boring radio show my dad liked pouring from the speakers in the living room.

Christy shrugged. "Only when I'm not blasting music or watching TV." She speared another tater tot and dunked it in ketchup.

"Or making a milkshake in the blender," Jenny said, reappearing and sitting down across from me. Her accent was like a Sunday afternoon in June, warm and unhurried.

"Or singing at the top of my lungs," Christy added.

"Or playing clarinet," Jenny said with a laugh.

Christy pulled her long, blond hair over one shoulder, her eyes twinkling. "I'm the noisiest person in my house by a landslide."

"Not me!" Jenny said, tilting her head toward her brother. "He walks like an elephant and farts a lot," she said, not bothering to lower her voice and not signing along, either. But she got smacked by her brother anyway. She rolled her eyes. "Too bad he's good at lipreading."

After dinner, from the front lawn, Mrs. Robertson signed for us to come home when the lights went on. I know because Christy translated. Mrs. Robertson picked up a hose and started watering the bushes; several other neighbors were doing the same. Christy, Jason, Jenny, and I pedaled away into the evening, Christy and I on the parents' bikes. The seat was raised so high on mine that I had to pedal on tippy-toe.

The air in Charlotte was the same temperature as my body; it'd been a stiflingly hot and muggy day, but it was starting to cool off.

Jason took a right turn and the rest of us followed, riding down the centers of the wide, paved streets, winding and weaving in incomplete figure eights, lazily floating toward the side

of the road when cars went by. We ended up in one of Jason's friends' driveways, barely stopping our bikes before hopping off and dropping them to the concrete.

For the next few hours, we hung out with kids we'd probably never see again in our lives. We all had a love of Kick the Can in common, and sometimes that's enough to feel like friendship on a summer night.

BACK AT THE Robertson house, Jenny moved to Jason's bottom bunk, so Christy and I got Jenny's room to ourselves. Christy padded across the thick coral carpeting to the bed where her duffel was, unzipping it and digging through in search of a sleep shirt.

"You did really well today," she said, meaning our daytime performance at a retirement home. "Especially 'Hard Knock Life.'"

"Thanks," I said, my cheeks turning pink, trying to avoid looking at her as she yanked off her tank top and shorts. "The residents were really sweet. I always want to, like, try to . . . um . . . you know, do a good job for them."

"They *were* sweet!" Christy said, turning to face me in her oversized tee. "I love when we perform at retirement homes. They're always so, like, genuine and enthusiastic!" She knotted her hair high on her head with a scrunchie. "Why aren't you getting ready for bed?"

"Uh... oh yeah," I said, standing up and unzipping my own bag.

With her toiletries in tow, Christy went to the bathroom connecting the two Robertson kids' rooms and locked the door that led to Jason's bedroom, but she didn't even shut the door on Jenny's side before sitting down to pee.

I turned away and put my nightshirt on over my clothes, then undressed underneath, pulling my tank top and bra out through the holes for the neck and right arm. Kids on the cast who'd been traveling a long time always changed in front of one another, but I wasn't used to it yet.

When Wes and I had sleepovers, I usually just face-planted onto the bed without changing, washing up, or brushing my teeth, but I joined Christy in the bathroom after she finished, flushed, and waved me over.

I pulled my hair high on my head like Christy's, taking the cold cream she offered, smearing white paste all over my forehead, cheeks, and chin. It felt like whipped cream cheese, smelled like spicy menthol, and made my skin tingle.

Christy held her fist near her shoulder and pretended to stab a fake knife as she whispered creepily, "Kill kill kill, mom mom mom."

I took a step away from her. She burst into laughter.

"Not a *Friday the 13th* fan?" she asked, looking at herself in the mirror, tilting her head to the side. "I guess we do look more like Michael Myers anyway."

"I watched *The Exorcist* once," I said, feeling like I needed to redeem myself.

"Wow, really?" Christy asked, soaking her washcloth under the faucet and starting to wipe off the face cream. "That one's too scary for me."

"Okay, fine," I admitted, too distracted by wiping my damp washcloth across my forehead to really think about what I was saying. I just . . . spoke. "Wes and I snuck in and saw one scene when Kris and Holly were babysitting us, and we basically ran away screaming." Christy laughed, actually snorting when I added, "Don't tell anyone, but I peed my pants a little."

"I totally would have, too! I actually did once, in front of a boy I liked, when my friend made me laugh while we were jumping on a trampoline!"

"What?" I asked, laughing so hard tears popped into my eyes. "What did you do?"

"Covered my waist with my sweatshirt and made up a story about needing to go home."

"That's so embarrassing!"

"The worst!" With only half her face cleared, Christy turned to look at me. "You know, you're pretty rad to hang out with, Stevie. I don't think I've ever heard you talk this much. You should talk more!"

"Yeah, yeah," I said, concentrating on my face.

I wanted to explain to Christy that it wasn't that simple.

That when I was feeling uncomfortable and like an outcast, worrying about how the words might get jumbled if I dared to speak, it wasn't like I could flip a switch and make it better. And it wasn't like I *chose* to feel comfortable around some people and not others. It was all just me, and it was frustrating and embarrassing.

But not tonight.

Tonight had been good.

Tonight, without even thinking about it, I'd shown my true colors to Christy. After brushing our teeth, we got in bed and Christy switched off the lamp. The room was pitch-black, and I thought we'd just go to sleep, but Christy kept the conversation going—with a surprising series of questions.

"So, like, what's up with your brother?" she asked.

"What do you mean?" I asked quickly and kinda defensively. Had Joey broken his promise and spilled the beans to Christy about Brandon's seizure?

"Oh, nothing," she said in a singsong voice that sounded higher than normal. "I just mean, like, what's he been up to this summer and stuff?"

What?

Warily, I said, "Normal junk, I guess."

"Like . . ." she prompted.

What the heck? Are you asking me if Brandon's planning to play football even though he's probably keeping seizures secret from

our parents? Are you a secret spy for the chaperones? Is that why you get all the good parts?

What are you even talking about, brain?! She gets the good parts because she's awesome!

"He likes music?" I asked back at her.

"What kind of music does he listen to?"

I said the first singer I thought of, who was definitely not one of Brandon's current favorites, but instead one we'd loved as little kids.

"Kenny Rogers."

"Brandon listens to . . . Kenny Rogers?" Christy asked.

"All the time," I said, nodding in the dark.

"You mean the country singer with that *know when to hold 'em* song?"

Our dad loved Kenny Rogers. "'The Gambler,' yep," I said, amused thinking of what Brandon would say if he were a fly on the wall right now. "He also really loves 'Lady.'"

"Wow, I never knew he liked country music."

"Loves it," I said, now just giddily messing with my brother for no reason other than the fact that I was happy Christy didn't seem to be talking about sports or epilepsy. Except then . . . "Why are you asking about Brandon?"

"Oh, just, like, I . . . some years I make people things . . . uh," Christy said, sounding like . . . me? She cleared her throat. "Sometimes I make people presents after tour is what I mean,

and I was thinking of making Brandon a mixtape, but I don't have any country music, so I probably won't."

"Oh," I said, wondering if she'd make *me* a present after tour, my thoughts focused on that instead of what my mouth was doing. That's why I didn't catch myself before saying, "Who knows what Brandon really likes right now—he's being kind of weird and secretive anyway."

"Really?" she asked, and I wished I could rewind my words. But then she said, "Sometimes brothers do that. Mine did. I get it."

"I didn't even know you have a brother."

"For sure," she said. "He's way older, though. His name is Randy." She forced a laugh. "We used to be close, but then he turned into a stuck-up jock and left for college, and now I never see him or talk to him except for over holidays."

"That's sad."

"It's a bummer for sure," she said. "Randy and I, we were, like, bonded because we're not deaf. I used to tell him everything, and he'd walk me home from school every day and, like, look out for me." She was quiet for a few seconds before asking, "Stevie, can you keep a secret?"

I flipped on my side to face her even though neither of us could see each other. Christy Hutchinson was going to tell me a secret! I tried to sound calm when I answered, "Totally."

"You can't tell anyone." I heard the rustling of her covers as she shifted to her side, too.

"I promise. I'm an exceptional secret-keeper." I thought of

my secret crush, and Wes's, and decided it wasn't a lie.

"Okay," Christy said. "The secret is that I like to sing. Like, a lot. And I mean, like, not to brag, but I'm kind of good."

"Rad! But why . . . why is that a secret?"

"I don't want to hurt my dad's feelings," she admitted. When I didn't say anything, she added, "My dad wasn't born deaf; he got really sick in his twenties and lost his hearing. But he used to sing, and I don't want to make him sad by doing what he can't."

"That's sad," I said.

"I don't mean to, like, bum you out," Christy said. "But the reason I brought it up is Randy's the only person in my family who's ever heard me sing, and now I don't have that, you know?"

"Yeah," I said even though I could never really understand what it was like to be different from your parents in such a big way. "That must feel lonely."

"That's a perfect word for it," Christy said before she got quiet again. Then suddenly she said, "Gag me, sorry for being such a downer!"

"You're never a downer," I reassured her. "You always make everyone feel happy."

"That's so sweet," Christy said. "Thanks, Stevie. It's really nice talking to you about this stuff." She shifted around on her bed to get comfortable.

"I think so, too," I said, rolling onto my back, smiling big.

"You should, like, talk to Brandon, though," Christy said before yawning. "I didn't with Randy, but I wish I would have."

"Okay," I said, catching her contagious yawn, feeling the pull of sleep. Jenny's bed was, like, mega comfortable. "I'll do it tomorrow."

"Okay," Christy said, yawning again.

Then it was morning.

21.

WE LEFT CHARLOTTE with the rising sun, Margo flooring it down Interstate 85 through the Carolinas and into Georgia, the Winnie shuddering from the speed.

"I hope we don't blow a tire," I said, chin on my fist, watching the white lines on the pavement get sucked under like dirt into a brand-new vacuum.

"Me too." Wes turned a page of *Dragon*. "Did you know that Cheyenne flooded the day after we left? It was so bad cars were underwater up to their windows."

"Who told you that?" I asked.

"I called my dad collect last night," Wes said like it was nothing, but it was something. His dad didn't live at home, or come

around much, or call on Wes's birthday some years. I was surprised he'd accepted the call at all. "He said we could go fishing before school starts."

Wes didn't even like fishing. He told me he always tried not to catch anything because he felt so bad for the fish.

"That's awesome," I said, trying to sound positive.

"Yeah, totally," he said. In our silence, we both pretended like we thought the fishing trip might happen.

"Did you, like, talk to Tuesday before we left this morning?" I asked, changing the subject.

Wes shook his head, still looking glum. "Not really. I gave her some gum and she said thanks and that's it."

I didn't like that not even an interaction with Tuesday could make his eyes sparkle today. Quietly, I said, "You know my dad would take you fishing if you wanted."

"I hate fishing."

"I know, I'm just saying he would if you wanted."

"I know."

One difference between me and Wes was that I hadn't talked to my parents in . . .

"What's the date?"

"August thirteenth," Wes muttered.

. . . fourteen days, but I knew that they loved and missed me, while Wes had talked to his dad just the day before but didn't know the same. It wasn't fair, but it was a fact.

Margo suddenly stopped the Winnie because Kimberly Erikson was a gnarly shade of carsick green, and Margo didn't want her to puke in the bathroom on board because then the whole Winnie would smell like vom, and we had a long day of driving ahead.

We pulled over at a gas station, and Mrs. Johnson, who seemed pumped to be able to mother someone who needed her instead of getting ignored by Amy, fed Kimberly ginger ale and saltines to turn her a normal color again. People stood in line for the dirty restrooms and restocked their candy supplies.

I watched through the door of the convenience mart as Wes went over to where Margo was squeegeeing bugs off the Winnie's windshield. She saw him coming with just enough time to turn, drop the squeegee, and open her arms.

Wes's expression must have told his mom that he needed the hug of the century, so that's what Margo gave him. He relaxed into her, and she stroked the back of his head, and I was thankful that he had one parent who could love enough for two.

WHEN KIMBERLY WAS a normal color again, back on board, Margo made Wes and me give Kimberly the loft bed to lie down in, and Courtney went up to take care of her. Little Josh sat down in the seat I was going to take next to Wes on the couch, squishing

Wes into the corner. The table seats were gone, so I ended up in a swivel chair next to Brandon.

He was pitched forward, digging in his backpack. As I started swiveling back and forth, he sat up, a library copy of *War With the Evil Power Master* in his hand, one of the Choose Your Own Adventure books.

I liked that he still read them; when we were younger and our mom dropped us off at the library while she went to the store, we'd race to the series section and sit on the floor in the stacks reading as much as we could before she came back.

"Yo," I said.

"What's up?" he said.

I shrugged. "I heard there's a new one out." I gestured to the book.

"Oh yeah? I'll hit the library when we're home."

"Cool beans," I said, nodding and swiveling, swiveling and nodding, thinking that the only way riding in the Winnie would be cooler was if Joey was on board, too. "You know that girl Jennifer who lives across the street?" Brandon nodded. "She made fun of me for reading *Vampire Express* last year. She said those books are for toddlers."

"Jennifer sounds like a moron," Brandon said, his eyes on his book.

"She's the one Mom wanted me to be friends with. As if."

"Huh. These books are rad. When have you ever read another book in second person? I'll tell you, you haven't—that's where."

I laughed quietly. "For sure."

Brandon leaned on his armrest and stretched his long, tan legs across the space between us, ignoring me as he read. I looked at this person who used to be my messy brother, always covered in dirt, now in a gleaming white polo with the collar popped, sandy hair perfectly combed, not much of a kid anymore but not an adult, either. And he had something wrong with his brain that made me want to protect him, but he was as big as our dad and hardly looked like he needed protecting.

He was still Brandon, and kind of *not* still Brandon, at the same time.

You're so confusing, I thought at him.

"I told Christy you like Kenny Rogers."

Brandon peered at me over his book. "That's warped."

"Psych," I said, taking it back even though it was true. But now that I had his attention again, I whispered, "Do Mom and Dad know?"

He dropped his book and leaned forward, whispering, "That I like Kenny Rogers?"

"Very funny," I said, leaning back hard against the chair and starting to swivel again. "You know what I mean." I wanted to shout, *I'M TALKING ABOUT YOUR SEIZURE!*

"I do, but I don't want to talk about it, and I wish you'd just be cool with that." He looked at me pointedly; I stared back. "It's *my* issue, Stevie. I'm dealing with it in my way."

"I just want you to be okay," I said softly.

"I am okay."

He smiled reassuringly, but it didn't reassure me. I felt like Brandon was basically saying there was no way he'd told our parents or any adults about the seizure, and it made me wonder if he'd had other seizures when I wasn't around that he hadn't told anyone about, either. And that was scary, because maybe he *shouldn't* be on tour. Probably he definitely shouldn't be on the football team. I wanted to say these things to him, but I also wanted to be cool about his wishes because it *was* his thing, not mine, and I wanted to keep a relationship with my brother and not lose him like Christy had lost hers.

That's why, even though I really wanted to ask more about how Brandon was feeling, the next question I asked was something else. "What's your favorite in the series?"

He answered immediately. "*Your Code Name Is Jonah.*"

"What's your second favorite?"

"*The Abominable Snowman.*"

"What's your th—"

"Steves," he interrupted, frowning at me. "You know there are, like, forty books, right?"

"Fine," I said with a sigh, and he went back to reading.

The kids on the couch, including Wes, were leaned on one another's shoulders, asleep, like tipped dominoes. The kids at the table were playing cards. I dug around in my bag for my Walkman, ejected the tape, and flipped it over. It was Journey,

and it technically belonged to Brandon, so I swiveled toward the window so he wouldn't see I'd borrowed it if he looked up.

I pressed play and listened to song after song that reminded me of Joey. It'd started raining, and the world outside the Winnie was gray and blurry—and by the time "Open Arms" came on, my eyeballs got blurry, too.

Hoping you'll see
What your love means to me
Open arms

Wiping my cheeks, I realized that maybe it was me that was making Joey act different sometimes. The night when Brandon had his seizure and the time we flirted in the dressing rooms— those were times when I was feeling confident. But at the stage in the forest, I was just regular.

Watching the miles go by, I wished I could be one of those people who seemed confident all the time. Brandon was like that. Christy was like that. Tuesday and Amy were like that. Joey was *definitely* like that.

I wanted to be like that—even just a little.

I wanted to be a little more of a star in regular life, not just onstage.

22.

I GOT MY chance to shine in Atlanta.

When I got back from sneaking outside to mail my latest Long-Distance Dedication, fifteen minutes before we went onstage at a community center auditorium, Courtney started throwing up.

"Courtney has food poisoning," Margo reported in the dressing room. Wes and I looked at each other and made vom faces. "Listen closely as I run through the understudies who are taking her parts. If you're assigned one, see Mrs. Johnson immediately to get a costume. We have thirteen minutes before showtime, and there's a big crowd, so no monkey business." Margo looked down at her clipboard. "Shane, you can sit out 'Summer Nights' since you won't have a partner. Holly, you're doing '9 to 5' with

Robyn and Christy. Tuesday, you're taking the lead in 'Fame,' and Stevie, you're taking Tuesday's part . . ."

Tuesday and I looked at each other. She was beaming, and I felt like I'd need the stall in the bathroom next to Courtney. Sure, I was officially an understudy for "Fame," but I'd never actually *performed* it.

"I can't do this," I whispered to Wes. "She has to put someone else in it."

"You can for sure do this," Wes whispered. "You know it. I've seen you at rehearsals."

"That's not the same."

"Want me to sit on the edge of the stage?" He smiled like he was joking.

"We're not six anymore," I said, even though it would have been great to have Wes sitting on the edge of the stage like when we were little, offering moral support just by being there.

Tuesday was waving me over, probably to give me tips about her part.

"Oh god," I said.

"Good luck," Wes said, and I left him behind.

RIGHT BEFORE THE song started, I got that feeling like I had to pee super bad, but there was nothing to do about it, so I stood tall and smiled big.

The movie *Fame* was about teenagers at a performing arts school in New York, so kids spent the intro beats of the number acting like they were studying drama, music, or dance. Kimberly, who'd been the one about to throw up from carsickness the day before but was fine now, played air guitar with Christy; Little Josh, his cousin Robert, and Wes's sister Kris acted like they were in a play; and Amy and I pretended to be ballerinas. Then Tuesday began lip-synching like she'd written the song herself.

Baby, look at me

And tell me what you see

During the chorus, we all stepped into staggers and fake-sang together about living forever and making people remember our names.

Fame!

In the movie, a New York City taxi driver blasts the song from his cab radio. The art school kids come out and dance, blocking traffic with their high kicks and twirling on top of cars. Our star boxes weren't cars, but I imagined they were—and that I was at art school in New York, dancing my heart out in a traffic jam.

The hardest part of the number was when the lyrics say the word "remember" a bazillion times in a row and Amy and I had to keep doing pirouettes through all of it—because we were supposed to be, like, professional teenage dancers and stuff. Since I had only met Mikhail Baryshnikov and wasn't actually him myself, mine weren't the prettiest pirouettes, but I didn't fall—and I stepped

out of the turns just in time to make way for Brandon to launch Kris into the air right when the song hit a high note.

I glanced at Margo, who was beaming at me, so I knew I'd done all right.

When the number was over, right after we'd cleared the stage, Tuesday rushed over and smashed me into a bear hug. Then she grabbed my shoulders and shook them as she said, "You did so awesomely good!"

I couldn't help but laugh.

"You really did, Stevie!" Christy said behind her. "You killed the turns."

"They were righteous!" Brandon said, and Christy nodded enthusiastically, agreeing with him.

They were all still talking about it when we made it back to the dressing room, and when Joey heard, he gave me a thumbs-up.

All the praise and attention made my face burn.

"Thanks, du-dudes," I said awkwardly before busying myself with changing out of my borrowed "Fame" costume and into my orphan outfit for "It's the Hard Knock Life," struggling so hard to contain my smile that my face literally hurt.

THE REST OF the performance was radical, like when there's an unexpected snow day off from school when there's supposed to

be a test. It was as if maybe everyone hadn't expected Atlanta to be so great, but then it was one of our favorite shows.

The top hats were overflowing with donations, and Courtney had stopped barfing. The chaperones were going to take us for pizza, and no one was more excited about that than Courtney. There was awesome energy in the air as we bounced down the community center hallway from the stage to the dressing room.

Then Wes did something shocking.

"I'm a bard," he said, a determined look on his face.

"Okaaaaay," I said, scratching my cheek where the makeup was especially caked on.

"Little Josh says bards are the least exciting, but they're cunning. It's, like, way hard to be a bard. They're charming! They're likable!"

"Did you hit your head?" I checked over my shoulder to make sure no one else was listening. No one was behind us.

Wes made me jump when suddenly he looked my way, dark brown eyes serious. "I'm totally inspired by how you're doing all this stuff so you can tell Joey you like him! I'm going to tell Tuesday I like her, too."

"You've been saying that for months," I said with a tsk. "Years? Decades?"

"No, for reals, I'm really going to this time."

"Sure."

Ahead, Tuesday and Amy had their heads tipped together in conversation, Tuesday giggling.

I was mid-sentence. "... really need to think of how you're ..."

Wes suddenly put on the brakes, so I stopped talking and walking, too.

"Tuesday," he said, loudly enough for her to turn around.

"What are you doing?" I whispered.

"What's up, Wes?" Tuesday asked.

"I told you I was going to," he whispered to me, then, to her, "Can you come here?"

I froze like a possum in a spotlight, trying not to draw attention to myself. Tuesday waved for Amy to head back to the dressing room with the others.

"What, like, *right now*?" I whispered.

Wes nodded once without looking at me. He sucked in enough air to fill his entire body, then let it out slowly. I held my breath.

Tuesday stopped in front of us, looking at Wes, then me, then Wes again, with her light eyes and barely-there freckles and just very *Tuesday* way of being in the world.

"I have something to tell you," Wes said.

"I should go," I said.

"No," Wes said, quickly putting his hand on my forearm to stop me. "Stay," he whispered. "Strength in numbers. Sit on the side of my stage."

"This is so weird," I whispered back. He squeezed hard, then dropped his hand. "Fine," I whispered sharply.

"What are you guys talking about?" Tuesday asked, tilting her head curiously.

"This is . . ." Wes began before stopping. He glanced at me; since I was being forced to be there like a giant third wheel, I went ahead and nodded my encouragement. Eyes back on Tuesday, he said, "I want to tell you . . ." He cleared his throat; the older kids' voices faded away as they disappeared into the dressing room. The hallway was quiet.

Tuesday waited patiently, blinking at Wes, a small smile on her lips.

Finally, Wes blurted, "I like you, okay?"

Tuesday laughed a little, sounding more like she was surprised or nervous than like she was making fun of him. Wes shifted in his star sweatshirt and black pants. I'm sure he felt awkward, but at least it was out there.

"That's nice of you to—" Tuesday began.

Amy popped her head out of the dressing room and shouted, "Margo says to hurry up!"

"Okay," Tuesday called back. She looked at Wes, then me, then Wes again. "Maybe we should . . ."

"Talk later?" Wes said quickly.

"Yeah," Tuesday said. "No offense to Stevie, but maybe . . ."

"When I'm not around," I quickly filled in the blank.

"I see in hindsight that might have been a better choice," Wes said before all three of us started laughing.

"Come on!" Amy shouted.

"We'd better . . ." Tuesday said.

"We'll be right there," Wes said.

Tuesday nodded, then turned and bounced her compact self down the hall, leaving me next to my best friend, who, as soon as Tuesday was gone, melted to the floor like his limbs had turned to nacho cheese.

"Why did I do that?" he asked with a groan.

"Because you're a bard," I said, sitting down on the carpet next to him and folding my legs into a pretzel. "And bards are cunning. They're smart and charming."

I was proud of Wes no matter what happened next, and I told him so.

We stayed like that, in the middle of the community center hallway, until he felt like he could walk again.

23.

THE WEDNESDAY OF the third week of tour, at a mansion in Jacksonville, Florida, everything changed.

Once again, I was assigned to stay with Joey, and I was on cloud nine riding home from the church where we performed. A larger-than-usual group was assigned to go home with the Hayes family, so I assumed they had a big house.

"Big house" was the understatement of the century.

We pulled off the main road and stopped at a gate. Mr. Hayes, which he pronounced in a slow drawl like he had all the time in the world to say his name, punched in a code, and the gate eased open. We made our way to the circular drive, where

there was a fountain with three huge spouts in front of what Mrs. Hayes called "home, sweet home."

Amy was next to me, and I decided to just strike up a conversation with her like I would with Wes or Brandon—and now even Christy or Tuesday. I knew I'd never get comfortable talking to people if I didn't just talk to people.

"The next time I play M.A.S.H., I'm, like, totally picturing this as the mansion," I whispered.

She nodded and whispered, in her superfast way of talking, "They're definitely millionaires."

We're having a conversation!

"Must be," I said, squinting up at the second-floor balconies. Plural. "I would *not* want to have a chore list at this house."

Amy laughed—she actually laughed! It wasn't loud or even very long, but it was a laugh. I felt so proud of myself. I couldn't wait to tell Wes.

We got out of the car and waited while the other carload got out, too.

Amy said, "This is how I pictured the hotel in *The Shining*."

"I don't know how you read that stuff," I said. "I'd be too scared."

"It's not real," she said with a shrug.

"Pretty bad, right?" Joey said, appearing next to Amy. We looked up at the massive entryway door, columns on either side. "It's sick!"

"*So* sick," I agreed, giddy that I got to stay in the same house

as Joey—now even more so since we got to stay together in an actual mansion, hopefully not the haunted kind. And he seemed to be in a mismatched-socks-Joey kind of mood, maybe because I was being... less awkward? More talkative? Something. Anyway, it seemed promising.

Inside, there was a crystal chandelier hanging high over the entryway that would most likely kill you if it fell while you were standing under it. The wood floors were polished to a slippery shine, and twin stairways curved up to the second floor, one right and one left. I wondered if you were supposed to walk up one and down the other, or if you could use whichever one you felt like. I didn't know the rules of mansion living.

The oldest of the three Hayes boys showed Amy and me to the room we'd share and asked if we wanted to go swimming. Since it was still around ninety billion degrees out, with one gazillion percent humidity, we basically had on our swimsuits before he'd finished the question.

With towels wrapped around us, our bare feet making smudge prints on the perfect floors, Amy and I tiptoed through the house toward French doors leading to the back patio. There, we found a pool almost as big as the one at the community center back home. If I had this in my backyard to practice in, I'd be unstoppable during swim season.

"That's it, I'm asking to be readopted," Amy said, tucking one side of her black hair behind her ear.

"I'll be your new sister," I said, giggling, mesmerized by the

shimmering bean-shaped aquamarine water lit from below, rippling with rollicking movement from the Hayes boys, Little Josh, Joey, and Christy! I hadn't realized she'd been in the other car.

Amy was still thinking about how to be readopted. "All they have is boys. I'm sure a couple of daughters would be good. But the chores."

"True," I agreed. "But the pool."

"The pool," Amy breathed.

Smells of cut grass, sweet flowers, and watermelon slices filled my nose. And the chlorine! I couldn't wait to get in, wondering when the last time was I'd gone swimming at night. I pinched myself to make sure I wasn't dreaming. Wes said once he'd pinched himself *in* a dream, so I wasn't sure the test was accurate, but I did it anyway.

Joey dove underwater, and I watched his blobby, blurry form swim along the bottom of the pool before he broke through the surface, laughing, whipping his head to the right and his soggy hair with it. He noticed us lurking near the doors.

"You guys took, like, forever," he called. "Get in, the water's righteous!"

"Hurry up!" Little Josh called.

"Yeah, you guys!" Christy said, beaming like a happy seal. Her blond hair looked dark when it was wet and slicked back off her face like that.

"Last one in is a rotten egg," I said, dropping my towel on a lounge chair.

"Rad suit," Amy said, not trying to cover up her obvious surprise.

I looked down at my strapless, hot-pink-and-royal-blue two-piece, which was cut low on the belly and high on the thighs. I'd bought it with babysitting money right before we left and hadn't worn it until now.

"Thanks, Amy," I said, blushing, meaning it big-time.

It's funny how a simple compliment can make you feel like you can do anything, even strut across a pool deck in a bikini in front of your crush. And that's just what I did.

Even though I had a pretty awesome dive, I didn't want to show off, so I started down the steps of the shallow end of the pool as Amy jumped from the edge, shouting, "Cannonball!" and splashing everyone nearby. We decided to play Marco Polo because that's what you did in pools, even mansion ones, apparently. The middle Hayes brother went first.

"Marco!" he called, his eyes closed, turning in circles.

"Polo!" we all called back.

"Marco," he called again, leap-gliding to the left, landing dangerously close to Amy. She ducked out of the way like a Ninja Turtle.

"Polo!"

Amy dove and disappeared, resurfacing at the opposite end of the pool. I gave her a surprised look, and she smiled devilishly. Who knew Amy was part dolphin like me? I liked that we had that in common.

I planned my next move from the deep end, gripping the wet concrete with raisin fingers, my hair slicked back off my face. I was a good swimmer but wanted to keep watch, so I dog-paddled across at the corner when Marco got too close.

Joey miscalculated a dive and ended up an arm's length from the kid who was Marco. In seconds, Joey was tagged "it." He swam to the center and closed his eyes, giving all of us time to reposition ourselves. I used the seconds to stare at his bare shoulders, smooth and strong.

Drool.

Unlike the Hayes kid, Joey searched for his victims underwater, launching himself into the air like an orca, then diving under, arms stretched out wide, ready to pull a Polo under. It was thrilling when once, his fingertip grazed my knee; I got away but kind of wished I hadn't.

Amy, Little Josh, and I got stuck in a shallow-end corner, and I was sure we were goners, but Joey the orca abruptly shifted his path and ended up closer to Christy. He was barely above water when he shouted, "Marco!"

"Polo!" we said in unison, Christy trying to make a break for it, but Joey anticipated her move. He dove under, and a second later, Christy was yanked underwater, too, gleefully screaming until she had to close her mouth or drink pool.

Everyone busted up, Amy maybe the loudest—I'd never heard her laugh that hard. Joey and Christy resurfaced, gasping for air and cracking up at the same time, brushing water and

waterlogged hair out of their faces, and slyly wiping their noses in case of pool boogers.

The oldest Hayes boy called time-out to go to the bathroom, and Little Josh, Amy, and the youngest Hayes went to scarf some watermelon. Next to me, the middle Hayes boy said, "Time me," and dove into an underwater handstand, his feet poking out above him, staying upside down for long enough for me to worry before he popped up, smiling, asking how many seconds it was.

"Ninety-seven," I said, turning to swim toward the stairs on my own watermelon-retrieval mission. Just then, something caught my eye.

Joey and Christy were treading water in the deep end, heads gently bobbing with the motion of flipper feet and swishy hands under the surface. Christy said something that made Joey do his howl-at-the-moon laugh, chin to the dark sky cluttered with bright stars.

They were only an arm's length apart, which I might have written off as nothing if I hadn't seen Joey reach out of the water and free a clump of hair that was stuck to Christy's cheek.

Then suddenly he burst forward like someone had shoved him from behind and planted a peck on Christy's cheek where the hair had been. I stared in horror as he ducked under the water and swam toward the shallow end.

Christy kept treading water, her back to me, so I couldn't see her expression. But as I watched the effortless, edgeless blob of Joey glide under the water, jealousy crept through me, from my

pool-scraped toes to my bruised shins to my gurgling stomach to my racing heart to my blazing-hot tomato face.

"What's up, Finnegan?" Joey asked as he surfaced, tone like nothing had happened. Like he hadn't just *kissed* Christy Hutchinson right in front of me, the girl he'd been maybe flirting with all tour. I didn't answer.

As Joey dragged his soggy self up the steps, he looked me up and down, then, eyes on mine, said, "Rad suit."

"Thanks," I whispered.

He nodded, hesitated, then continued up the steps, brushing my shoulder with his as he went by. "You look pretty fine there, Finnegan."

My mouth dropped open, but he didn't see.

Joey DeLeon had just kissed Christy, looked at me like I was a prime rib, and told me I was fine in the same minute. I felt like I was going to spontaneously combust from confusion.

I faked a stomach cramp and rushed inside, up the left side of the grand staircase—whether it was meant for down or up, I didn't care—and into the guest bathroom, locking myself inside. I changed into pajamas and threw my suit into a wad in the corner, mad at it for some reason.

I slumped against the door and hugged my knees and sobbed.

I missed everything.

I missed Wes, even though I'd see him tomorrow. It wasn't cool to say, but I missed home—not exactly my parents but just my regular life in my regular-sized house and sleeping in my

regular bed and eating cereal with Brandon in the mornings instead of worrying about whether he was going to have a seizure while staying with strangers in Florida.

I missed the afternoon rainstorms in Wyoming that washed everything clean, making it smell fresh and new afterward. I missed riding my bike wherever I wanted to go instead of driving to unfamiliar places and doing the same show over and over and over again.

I missed the real Joey, the mismatched-socks Joey who worried about Brandon and kept his secret and who I'd had a crush on for two years, not the version of him who was maybe a little bit of a jerk like Shane or even some big flirt who liked every girl but only loved himself.

"I want to go home," I said to no one.

It made me cry harder.

Sometimes that's what happens when you say the truth out loud.

24.

THURSDAY, AUGUST 15, 1985

Dear Mr. Kasem,

My name is Stevie Finnegan, and I've been sending you Long-Distance Dedications all month for a boy named Joey. If you were planning to play one on the radio this Saturday, <u>please do not do that, Mr. Kasem</u>.

He kissed someone else, and it's someone radical, and if she likes him back, then there's just no hope for me at all.

If you have any of my letters, please just rip them up.

Sincerely,
Stevie Finnegan

25.

SINCE WE FOUND ourselves somewhere new every one or two days, and since heartbreak added minutes to the hours, the August I'd lived so far felt like a year when, in reality, we were at the end of week three. Wes and I were still assigned to the Winnebago on the way to Orlando, Florida, but to pour salt in my gaping wound, Joey joined us when Kimberly felt carsick again, and Margo made her switch to the Bronco. Joey had volunteered, making me question his motives.

"Buttface," I muttered as I saw him strutting across a high school parking lot, the blacktop vibrating from the heat.

"What'd you say?" Wes asked from the swivel chair opposite mine, his eyes on *Dragon*.

"Nothing," I said.

I hadn't had a moment alone with Wes to tell him yet—not that I really wanted to. Admitting that Joey had kissed Christy would be admitting that I liked someone who didn't like me back—and that was humiliating.

I kicked myself for not telling Wes when he hopped up when he saw Joey stepping on board, claiming he'd rather sit on the couch with Robyn. The eyebrows he waggled at me when Joey wasn't looking told me Wes was just trying to be nice, but right then I didn't want to be anywhere near Joey.

"Hey, Stevie!" Joey said enthusiastically after taking the empty seat. "Do you know how to play Rummy?"

He already had a deck of cards in his hand. "We were playing in the Bronco." He looked at me expectantly, smiling with straight teeth that never needed braces, perfect skin, not a pimple in sight. He was beautiful.

"Not really," I said. "Sorry."

"That's okay, I'll teach you." He wasn't exactly giving me a choice in the matter.

"Okay, thanks," I managed, wishing I could get out my Walkman and listen to a sad mixtape, but knowing I'd probably start crying about Joey right in front of Joey, so cards were a better option.

The RV roared to life as I watched Joey shuffle the deck, his long fingers making the cards zipper together with ease. He dealt us each ten cards, then put the stack in the middle and turned

over one card next to it. He explained the rules, which I only half heard, because I was distracted by his full lips with a crack in the middle of the bottom one.

You were supposed to kiss me, not Christy.

"You go first," Joey said, looking at me with deep brown eyes that always sparkled even if he was tired. "Draw from the stack or take the upcard."

I hesitated, suddenly wanting to tell him. Wanting to say, aloud, *I like you.* Wanting to tell him that I liked how he could keep a secret. That he admitted he didn't know what to do when Brandon was in trouble—that he immediately got help. I liked that he had a dog he loved. I liked how it sounded when he crunched ice, and how he smelled when he stood close to me. I liked that when we performed together it felt like it was just us, him and me. I wanted to tell him that when I closed my eyes at night, I could still see his face as clear as when he was right in front of me, because I thought it was the most perfect face I'd ever seen on a boy. I wanted to tell him that I fell out of a tree the first time I saw him and knocked the wind out of my chest, and ever since then, I felt breathless when he looked at me. Like he was right now.

He knitted his thick eyebrows together. "Everything copacetic, Stevie?"

"Huh?"

"You seem kinda . . ." He tilted his head, scratching his chest, searching my face. He might have looked concerned, or maybe I just wanted him to.

I opened my mouth to say it, to tell him everything. "The thing is that I—"

The Winnebago hit a curb going around a corner, tipping too much to the left, making a couple of kids scream. Joey caught the stack of cards before it slid off the table; duffel bags dropped down from the loft over the driver's seat. The Winnie slammed back to the ground.

"Sorry!" Margo yelled from the front. "Everyone okay?"

We all yelled back that we were, but I wasn't, not at all.

I played three heart cards, hoping Joey would read into it, but he just tossed a seven on the pile, making my hearts disappear. We played the rest of the way to Orlando, and every glance at him hurt. The moment from before was gone; we were just two castmates killing time, him winning most of the rounds because my heart wasn't in it.

"Rummy," Joey said, laying down the last of his cards just after we went by the WELCOME TO ORLANDO sign.

I was defeated.

26.

AS AWFUL AS the ride was, there was no way to be unhappy at Walt Disney World. I guess that's why they call it the Happiest Place on Earth.

After the adults parked the caravan in the hugemongous lot and herded us to the gate, after we all impatiently waited while they figured out tickets and meetup times and places, Wes and I broke free from the rest of the Synchronicity cast and sprinted away, leaving everyone we knew and everything that was bothering us behind.

Whether Wes and Tuesday would turn into a couple remained to be seen—she hadn't brought it up again, and Wes said he sure as heck wasn't going to.

Wes hadn't mentioned his dad again.

Joey had kissed Christy, and I wanted to avoid both of them.

Brandon said he was okay, but I didn't know if he really was, and I didn't want to even begin to think about it if he wasn't.

But there Wes and I were, sneakers slapping on the Main Street blacktop, laughing as we dodged churro vendors and families in mouse ears and bunches of balloons, until we came to a screeching halt in front of a futuristic building, thunder rumbling inside.

"There it is," Wes breathed, awestruck.

"It's unreal," I murmured. "I think I'm dreaming."

Wes pinched me on the arm. "Ouch! Knock it off!"

"You're awake," he said with a laugh, dodging my smack.

I shoved him and took off running toward the entrance to Space Mountain, the roller coaster rumored by the lucky few kids back home who'd ridden it to be the raddest of all time.

Three rides in a row later, Wes and I strapped into the front coaster car. Clutching the handrail tightly, Wes shouted over the space, "Whoop, whoop, whoop" as we climbed up, up, up through pretend lightspeed, where they'd drop us once again off the top of a hill through blackness and stars and wonder.

"This is the raddest roller coaster of all time!" he yelled.

"This is the raddest day of all time!" I yelled.

"You're the raddest friend of all time!" he yelled.

I beamed at him just before we reached the top, shouting, "You too!"

And then we threw our arms in the air and fell off the edge of infinity through Walt Disney's version of space, crushing each other's rib cages on the sharp turns, belly laughing like never before, just Wes and me, me and Wes.

27.

I WAS SITTING on the carpet, messing with Courtney's Magic 8 Ball early the next morning at the hotel near Disney World. Courtney was in the shower, and perpetually carsick Kimberly Erikson was still asleep, sprawled sideways across the bed, limbs everywhere. Wes's sister Holly was by the vanity, curling her long, auburn princess hair.

    I felt young and awkward and kind of empty, sitting there in my new Mickey Mouse nightgown with ratty bedhead. Heartsick about Joey, my homesickness was amplified. I think we were actually farthest away right then—at least it felt like it. I wanted to call my mom, but sometimes when I heard her voice and I was already sad or having my period, both of which were true today,

the sound of it made me cry. I didn't want to cry in front of the older girls.

Instead, since I couldn't say them aloud or else Holly would hear, I thought questions at the Magic 8 Ball. It was magical, after all, so it shouldn't have had a problem reading my mind.

It's Saturday. Is Casey Kasem going to read one of my Long-Distance Dedications today?

I shook the ball and turned it over.

Ask again later

I blew out my breath, then thought the question again. Technically, it was later . . . than a few seconds ago.

Is one of my Long-Distance Dedications going to be read on AT40 today?

This time, it said:

Better not tell you now

"Thanks a lot," I said out loud accidentally. Holly glanced at me but didn't say anything; she just pulled free another section of hair to curl. She had on a boring white tank top but she made it look special.

I pulled my nightshirt over my knees, stretching it out, but I didn't care. I felt better like that, all of me squished under the fabric except my arms and feet. I probably would have sucked in my arms, too, had I not wanted the Magic 8 Ball to tell me how the day would go already!

I tried thinking some different questions at the plastic toy, rapid-fire.

Does Joey like Christy, or was he just messing around?

Concentrate and ask again

Did Joey ever like me? Does Christy like Joey back?

Reply hazy, try again

Are you the worst Magic 8 Ball ever made?

My sources say no

Just then, someone pounded on the door. Kimberly groaned and smashed a pillow against her face. "Go away!" she said, her words garbled.

"Can you see who's there?" Holly asked, looking at my reflection in the mirror, the hot iron sending up smoke from her hair. I worried she was going to burn it off.

"Sure," I said, dropping the Magic 8 Ball, growing legs again, and walking over to the door in what was now a Mickey Mouse muumuu. I flung open the door without checking the peephole first, trusting it was someone we knew.

I was right, but that someone looked totally goofy.

Wes's face was a little kid's drawing of a smiley face, his features huge and exaggerated, like they hurt.

"What's wrong with you?" I asked, frowning. "Why's your face stuck like that?"

"Who is it?" Holly called from the vanity.

"Your brother," I called back, staring at him, trying to figure him out.

I motioned Wes inside, and he followed, letting the heavy hotel door slam behind him and making Kimberly groan again.

Holly eyed him through the mirror. "What's up with you, Weasel? You look like a clown."

"I'm completely fine," he said in a strange voice I'd never heard before.

Kimberly threw the pillow off her face. "Why are you guys, like, the noisiest ever?" She propped herself up and frowned at Wes. "Holly, why does your brother look like he smiled and someone slapped him on the back and made it stay that way?"

"That's my question," Holly said, separating another strand of straight hair and wrapping it around the iron. I used to let my mom curl my hair, until she burned my ear one too many times, but maybe I'd ask Holly to do it sometime.

"Who looks like what?" Courtney asked, emerging from the bathroom in a cloud of steam, bangs flat and her private parts barely covered. Wes's expression didn't change; with three older sisters, he was used to being around half-naked girls.

"That." Holly gestured. "I mean, like, check him out."

"Maybe he's possessed," Kimberly said. "Wes, did you, like, sell your tiny toddler soul to the devil or something?"

"Hey now," Holly said, pulling a face at Kimberly. "Be nice to Weasel. He'll grow someday." She looked at her brother. "Why are you here anyway? Just to get razzed?"

"No, to tell you that Mom wants everyone in the ballroom," Wes said, the smile never fading. "She wants to rehearse the finale numbers because Ms. Freeman told her we messed them up in Jacksonville."

"Ohmigod," Courtney said, rolling her eyes. "That woman needs to get a life. And some clothes that aren't color coordinated!"

Courtney pulled underwear from her bag and started to shimmy into them under her towel. My eyes found the sprinkler spout on the ceiling, and Wes covered his with the smack of his palm to give her privacy. He still had the same painted-on grin that he'd had when he walked in.

"Courtney, you're going to make my brother fall in love with you," Holly said. "Cover yourself."

"I'm good, take your time," Wes said.

"Working on it," Courtney said.

"There are donuts," Wes added, eyes still covered.

"Well, why didn't you say that!" Kimberly said, throwing off the covers and messing up her already messed-up hair, then heading toward the door in her T-shirt and shorts, not even stopping to put on a bra.

Holly hurried to finish the last couple of curls, and by the time she was ready, Courtney was dressed. The second they were gone, Wes finally blurted it out, the reason for his perma-grin and general weirdness.

"Tuesday likes me back! I saw her at the vending machine, and she told me she was just waiting to tell me until no one else was around because it was, like, private, but oh my god, she likes me back!"

Jealousy flicked me hard on the earlobe, but a millisecond

later, all the right feelings were there, and I ran over to Wes and hugged him tight.

"This is the greatest news!" I said into his sharp shoulder. "And of course she likes you back."

"I'm so lucky!" he said, pulling away, his smile making me concerned for the future of his face. Would he ever *stop* smiling?

"Tuesday's the lucky one," I said, beaming back at him.

Because he may have looked like a scary clown, but what I said was true. Wes was the best.

Ms. Freeman had gone off somewhere, so Margo told us to chill in the ballroom with our donuts and wait until Ms. Freeman came back—then we'd rehearse the finale numbers that apparently were so sucky in Jacksonville. Everyone was still tired from the late night at Disney World, so instead of sitting at the big round tables scattered throughout the room, most everyone stretched out on the brown-and-tan floral carpeting.

Wes kept glancing over at Tuesday, who kept glancing back, and their budding eyeball romance was so cute I felt like I might vom.

Christy was clustered together with Brandon, Amy, and Tuesday, playing with a paper fortune-teller, and I wondered if she was hoping it would tell her about a bright future with Joey.

Now I felt like I might hurl for real.

As if that wasn't bad enough, Little Josh plugged in his boom box, but instead of starting a tape, he adjusted the radio dial until a familiar voice echoed through the high-ceilinged room. I had specifically not suggested to Wes that we ask Kris to stall again—but had she poisoned Ms. Freeman again anyway? We'd never told her our reason to want to stall before—did she think she was doing us a favor without knowing why?

"This is Casey Kasem in Hollywood. Thanks for joining me to count down the Top Forty hits of the nation this week on *American Top 40*—"

"Ohmigod," I groaned. "This can't be happening."

"It's radical!" Wes said. "If he says one of your dedications, everything will be out in the open!"

I still hadn't told him about Joey kissing Christy, so I was alone on Nervous Island.

Casey Kasem continued. ". . . top songs from the Atlantic to the Pacific, from Canada to Mexico, hot off the Billboard charts for the week ending August 17, 1985. In at number forty this week is . . ."

"Mötley Crüe!" Brandon guessed.

"'Dress You Up' by Madonna!" Shane shouted.

They were both wrong; it was "Lay It Down" by Ratt, and as most of the older boys started air guitaring along while squirming around on the floor and making super-weird instrument-playing faces, I majorly stressed out.

"This is a total nightmare," I said. "It's worse than that actual

nightmare I had about the gargoyles coming alive and chasing me through the streets of an abandoned Cheyenne."

"That's totally weird," Wes said. "But why's it a nightmare? If it happens, it'll be your dream come true."

"Not exactly." I looked at him seriously.

"What's going on?" He shifted so he was fully facing me.

Everyone was milling around, potentially overhearing, so I leaned forward and whispered quickly in Wes's ear.

"Joey kissed Christy at the host family's mansion in Jacksonville, and I didn't tell you because I'm so totally humiliated I might die right now."

I pulled back and we locked eyes, and instead of getting annoyed at me for keeping secrets or asking me a lot of questions that would make me relive the gag-me moment, Wes just said, "I'm sorry."

I sniffed hard when tears blurred the corners of my eyes.

"Don't make me cry."

"Lie down and look at the ceiling; your tears will get sucked back into your body," he instructed, tipping onto his back.

"I don't think that's real," I said, doing it anyway.

"Probably not." We were settled in a *V* shape with our heads together.

"What am I going to do?"

"For reals, don't worry," he said, sounding serious. "The dedications are never until at least halfway, and my mom will be back *way* before then."

"I've heard them early in the show," I protested.

"Yeah, but that's rare," Wes said reassuringly. "It's only if the dedication is actually one of the songs in the countdown."

"Not always," I said. He was trying, but I knew *AT40 way* better than Wes did.

Casey Kasem played a song called "Cry," then "There Must Be an Angel" by Eurythmics. I tried not to look at Joey when Annie Lennox sang the chorus because he totally was a completely gorg angel and—

He likes Christy!

"Make it stop," I whined, checking the ballroom door, hoping to see Margo and Ms. Freeman walking through.

Darn you, Ms. Freeman! Where are you? Debating over which monochrome outfit to wear today? It's okay if you don't match for once! Get in here already!

"You don't think your sister killed Ms. Freeman, do you?" I asked.

"I doubt it, but you never know," Wes said.

"I'm sorry I'm a downer when you just got great news."

"I'm sorry I got great news when you're sad."

We sighed in unison.

Everyone else was chill and happy, but the further Casey Kasem got into the countdown, the more my blood pressure rose. I felt like my heart was going to jump out of my chest every time a song ended, thinking the Long-Distance Dedication was up next. From the Pointer Sisters to Rick Springfield to Billy Joel,

my insides twisted and looped and tucked themselves tighter and tighter into knots. I dug my fingernails into my sweaty palms, listening, hoping.

"Invincible" by Pat Benatar started, and something about my state made the lyrics make sense to me right then. She sang about shattered dreams and screaming until you're satisfied.

My dream of Joey *had* been shattered. I *did* feel like screaming until I was satisfied—and that might take a long time of screaming, because I was pretty worked up!

"I love this song," I said, staring at the ceiling, not really caring if Wes was listening. "I'd love to perform this song. We should put it in the show."

"It's a little . . . angry . . . don't you think?"

"What's wrong with anger?" I snapped.

"Okay then," he said. "Don't bite my head off. I'm not . . . *him*." I looked at him sharply. "Sorry, but it's true."

"Duh," I said meanly, eyes back on the ceiling.

"It's not from a movie anyway," Wes said in a softer voice. "So we, like, couldn't add it to the show."

"Is so," I argued, just feeling like arguing, I guess. "It's from *The Legend of Billie Jean*."

"Never seen it."

I hadn't, either, but I didn't care. I liked the song. I liked the part about being invincible and facing the enemy. I liked the idea of not waiting for someone else to help you, of just doing what needed to be done yourself. It made me feel like maybe, the

next time I liked a boy, I might just walk up to him and tell him instead of trying to get a radio deejay to do it for me.

"Okay!" Margo shouted, rushing in with Ms. Freeman behind her. I was glad to see that Ms. Freeman, head to toe in orange, was neither sick nor dead. "We're back! Everybody on your feet!"

Relief washed over me as I sat up, knowing Margo would make Little Josh turn off the boom box, knowing I was saved. I hadn't exactly saved myself like the song said, but I was okay with it this time. I stood up and brushed myself off, feeling kinda invincible anyway.

I offered Wes a hand and pulled him to standing, then gave him a hug as an apology for temporarily being afflicted by jerkiness. He hugged back to tell me it was okay, he got it.

Like reanimating zombies, some of the cast was up, some sitting, and some still flat on the floor, everyone moving slowly and stiffly. Brandon had even fallen asleep. He looked peaceful, and I wondered if he hadn't slept the night before—and then I worried about him. I felt bad when Margo clapped her hands loudly and startled him awake.

Margo started saying something but interrupted herself mid-sentence and turned toward Mrs. Johnson to ask a question. They both turned toward Mr. Schneider to talk to him.

"This is taking forever," I groaned, stretching my arms overhead. I hadn't slept well the night before; I'd shared a bed with Courtney, and she kicked like an angry kangaroo.

Wes didn't say anything; he was looking at Tuesday again.

She was looking back. This was going to be a long last week of tour if all they were going to do was stare at each other.

"Invincible" ended.

Little Josh turned toward the boom box, probably to turn it off, but he didn't get there fast enough.

"This week's Long-Distance Dedication comes from a twelve-year-old named Stephanie, who goes by Stevie . . ."

Wes and I froze, snowmen, eyes round as buttons.

"No," I whispered.

"No way," Wes whispered back. He grabbed my hand instinctively. Now we were snowmen holding hands.

"What's going on?" Brandon asked, standing up, wearing a confused expression. "Did you send a dedication?"

Across the room, Tuesday, Amy, and Christy were looking at me curiously.

"Turn it off," Wes shouted at Little Josh, who didn't understand what he was saying. Or maybe he just wanted to hear the dedication.

Casey Kasem's voice broke through the hubbub. ". . . reads, 'Dear Mr. Kasem, I'm in a performing . . .'"

"Is that . . ." Christy asked, examining me. "Did you . . ." She stopped when she saw my face. "Stevie, what's wrong?"

You! I wanted to shout, but then felt guilty about it.

"'. . . touring the East Coast with . . .'" Casey Kasem went on.

"Turn . . . it . . . off!" Wes shouted at the top of his lungs.

"Shh!" a bunch of older kids snapped at him.

"Stevie, what did you—" Brandon began.

"Shhh!" the kids cut him off, too.

"'. . . reveal a crush to a boy named . . .'" Mr. Kasem read, probably thinking he was doing me a favor. Probably thinking he was doing what I wanted.

And then, celebrated national radio program host Casey Kasem, in his soothing, healing voice, wrecked my entire world.

He said it.

"'Joey.'"

"What?"

"Whoa!"

"No way!"

"Dude!"

My betraying eyes landed on Joey, as much as I wanted to look anywhere but at him. His face was deep red in humiliation. Shane was muttering a string of cut downs, shoving him and laughing, teasing Joey because clearly to Shane this was the most hilarious thing that had ever happened.

Joey looked at me with an expression that said all the bad things:

Why did you do this?

I'm totally embarrassed!

I would never like you like that.

How could you think this would end well?

At least that's what I heard.

I hid my face in my hands.

"'... please play for Joey the song 'Time After Time' by Cyndi Lauper . . .'" Casey Kasem continued, kids in the cast reacting with sounds from *oooh*s to groans to *ohmigod*s, and everything in between. "Stevie says, 'I like the part that talks about how if you fall, I will catch you, time after time, because I'd do that for Joey. And I hope he'd do that for me, too.' Now here, for Joey from Stevie, is 'Time After Time.'"

The song began, and the ballroom was otherwise silent, a sea of stunned teenagers and five adults who had no idea what to do with the rainstorm of awkwardness that'd just rolled in.

I ran.

28.

I SPENT TWO days in Margo-approved hiding in the hotel in Orlando.

Mercifully, Margo had given me her room after I'd hurled for real in the lobby bathroom, humiliation and heartbreak bringing up the jelly donut I'd inhaled. Margo moved her stuff to the Winnie and told everyone I wouldn't be performing at the high school on Saturday evening because I was sick. Then, when I faked sick on Sunday, too, she pretended to believe me, forcing the understudies to continue to do my parts at the performance at the Baptist church.

But we had to leave sometime, so Monday morning, the

beginning of the last week of tour, I emerged from the hotel, hiding my tearstained tomato cheeks behind the heart-shaped sunglasses I'd bought in the gift shop. I wore one of my favorite outfits to try to outdress my mood: a sleeveless white polo tucked into navy-and-white-striped blouson shorts.

"You look nice," Wes said when he saw me. "Feeling any better?"

He'd stopped by my sick bay as much as he could while still leaving time to stare at Tuesday. I got it, but it'd made me feel bad anyway. I wished that he'd just stayed the whole time. I didn't say that, though. I didn't want to make him feel guilty.

I shrugged. "I just don't want anyone to laugh at me."

"If it makes you feel better, I haven't heard anyone say, like, *anything* about it at all."

"They wouldn't say it to you," I said. "They know you're my BFF."

"Still."

I was assigned to the minivan with the Johnsons, and Wes to the Bronco, so we had to say goodbye for now.

"Only one more week," he said encouragingly. "Then back to normal."

"Yeah," I said, not sure normal would be better, but at least I wouldn't have to see Joey every single day when we got home. I hadn't seen his painfully perfect face since the ballroom, and even though I knew he was probably nearby, I kept my eyes on

Wes to avoid seeing Joey. In fact, my plan was to try to avoid him for the rest of the tour.

Wes hugged me goodbye, and, feeling like a breakable vase, I climbed into the wayback middle seat between Tuesday and Russell Gross, who had super-duper hairy legs that tickled mine, making me think there were spiders creepy-crawling up my calf. In the row in front of us, Shane's older brother, Trevor, sat between Wes's sisters, the twins, Kris and Holly.

It was a pretty neutral car assignment, all things considered. Every other kid in the van was older than me, Tuesday, just a year—but Russell, Trevor, and the twins were sixteen. Any one of them could have actually driven the van if Mr. Johnson had wanted them to. And all of them were, like, the chillest sixteen-year-olds. Unlike his sister, Wendy, who either didn't speak to me or was super rude, Russell had kind eyes and a calming vibe. And Trevor was the exact opposite of his brother, Shane, tall, fit, and . . . nice. There was no Christy. And more importantly there was no Joey. I wondered if Margo had put me here, with these specific castmates, on purpose.

"What'd you do by yourself all day yesterday?" Tuesday asked gently as Mr. Johnson revved the engine and adjusted the mirrors.

"Watched *Family Feud* and jumped on the bed, mostly," I said. "Until Ms. Freeman knocked on the adjoining door and made me stop." Margo had assigned Ms. Freeman to babysit me,

and now I knew what she looked like in hair rollers. "Oh, and I took a bubble bath." I screwed up my lips in thought. "I listened to my mixtapes." *While dancing dramatically and lip-synching along.* "And Margo brought me a ham sandwich when you guys got back. I don't really like ham, but it was okay."

"Well, the show wasn't the same without you," Tuesday said, giving me a small smile. "Don't tell her I told you, but Courtney's really bad at the 'Hard Knock Life' choreo. Kind of, like, the *worst.*"

I laughed a little. "I'm sure it was awesome. It's not like . . ." I didn't want to say what I was thinking and sound like a pathetic goober. But what was in my brain was, *It's not like I add anything to the show that's not already there without me.*

"I think Joey's a jerk for not saying anything," Tuesday whispered. Wes had filled her in on what'd happened with Christy. "Even if he . . . doesn't, like . . . feel the same way," she said softly, "it's still mega rude to just never say anything at all."

"Like, what would he say, though?" I asked.

"Like, thank you?" she asked back. "You went to a lot of trouble, and the least he could do is say thank you. It's nice to be liked, even if you don't feel the same way. Boys are idiots."

"Not all boys," I said, thinking of Wes.

"No, not all boys," she agreed, her light eyes sparkling like she was thinking of Wes, too. Jealousy pinched me, but I told it to bug off. As much as I was sad for me, I was trying hard to be happy for them.

We made it to the highway, and most people put on headphones and kicked back, but I just sat and stared, floating through the beginning of the seven-hour drive to Mobile, Alabama. The kids were all chill, but Mrs. Johnson was not: She kept yelling at Mr. Johnson for his driving, which was kind of funny and distracted me from my thoughts.

Since we were with the Johnsons, we were all wearing seat belts—gag me. Mrs. Johnson kept turning around and asking us if we still had them on.

"It's very important so you don't go through the windshield when Mr. Johnson crashes the car because he's tailgating so much," she said.

Mr. Johnson didn't say anything, but the back of his neck was bright red.

A little over halfway through the drive, everyone started to get antsy, so it was time for fuel. Tuesday passed around a box of M&M'S. I took a few, then hairy Russell did, then Tuesday stretched forward to hand the box to Kris. She took some, but when she passed it to Trevor, he didn't get a firm grip before Kris let go, so brightly colored chocolate deliciousness scattered across the floor of the van.

"Good going, butterfingers!" Kris said, quickly leaning over to see how many candies had spilled.

"Don't make a mess!" Mrs. Johnson said, not looking back at us. "The speed limit is sixty-five!" she shouted at her husband.

"We're not!" we all said in unison. Mrs. Johnson didn't seem to care about what we were or weren't doing back here, just that we were in seat belts.

"You spilled half the box," Holly said to Trevor.

"They're still good," Trevor said, shrugging. "Just scoop them up!"

"They are *not* still good," Kris and Holly said at the same time, both looking offended with their mismatched faces.

Trevor picked up a handful of floor M&M'S and inspected them. "Yeah, dudes, you're right. They're covered in dirt and pet hair and"—he looked closer—"sequins!"

"Dare you to eat them," Russell prodded, laughing. "Sequins and all."

"Ooooh, now you have to!" Tuesday chimed in. "You've been challenged!"

"As if!" Trevor said, looking over his shoulder and rolling his eyes at her. His big head was almost touching the ceiling. "That doesn't mean I automatically have to do it, Wednesday Addams."

"Really? You can't do any better than that?" Tuesday asked, laughing.

"Whatever, dude, alls I mean is you have no clue how dares work. You don't have to, like, automatically do a dare just because someone dares you. I'm *not* eating these. Barf me out!"

Tuesday glanced at me, and she must have seen something encouraging, like I was having fun listening to them, waiting

to see what would happen. And maybe I was. The next thing I knew, Tuesday turned up the volume.

"Chicken," she said. "You're afraid of a few germs?"

"Bite me," Trevor said. "I'm not doing it." He looked around. "Hey, Holls, toss me that empty cup. I'll put them in."

"What will you give me if I eat the dirty handful of M&M'S?" Tuesday asked confidently.

Kris, Trevor, and Holly all turned around from the middle row, surprise on their faces.

"I'll believe it when I see it," Kris said.

"You're going to get sick," Holly said, sounding concerned.

"Take them already," Trevor said. "They're melting all over my hand."

Tuesday quietly unbuckled and leaned up to take the M&M'S from Trevor's hand. He happily handed them over, wiping the melted color from his palm onto his shorts.

Russell laughed. "She's gutsier than you are, Trev."

"Fine by me," Trevor said.

Tuesday held the handful close to her mouth. "So? What do I get?"

"Don't do it," I said in a low voice.

"I'll be fine, Stevie," Tuesday reassured me.

"Why do I have to give you anything?" Trevor asked. "I didn't dare you to eat the dirty candy!"

"Yeah, but, like, you didn't take the dare and she did," Kris

said bossily. "So it's only fair that you give her a prize for doing it."

"Fair is fair," Holly said, her voice like sunshine.

"You guys suck," Trevor protested before sighing. "Fine, Tuesday, I'll owe you a favor."

"A *big* favor," Tuesday said.

"That's not even—"

"Yeah, dude, a big favor," Kris interrupted, obviously just getting a kick out of messing with Trevor.

Russell laughed quietly next to me. "I don't know how you got yourself into this mess, but I don't want to be walking in your shoes right now."

"I didn't do anything!" Trevor said, but he laughed, too. It was all just a game, making me feel lighter after worrying and hiding and hiding and worrying the past few days. "Okay, fine," he said finally, "I'll owe you a big favor, Tuesday. But nothing life-threatening!"

"Tuesday would never threaten your life, would she, dear?" Mrs. Johnson said. I hadn't realized she'd been listening. Lower, she added, "But Mr. Johnson might with his dangerous race-car driving."

Everyone busted up, and then Tuesday counted down, and I wondered if she'd really go through with it. Just as I started to think she might not, she shoved the entire handful of M&M'S, complete with all the nastiness from the floor, into her mouth.

Kris and Holly groaned in unison as Russell shouted, "Dude!"

Trevor watched in admiration as Tuesday quickly chewed a few times and swallowed, then opened her mouth wide to show that nothing was left.

"That was the easiest dare ever!" Tuesday said gleefully. "And I get a big favor!"

"Totally," Trevor said, laughing. "You earned it."

Tuesday looked at me conspiratorially, pushing her red frames up higher on her nose. Leaning close, she said, "I don't know when, and I don't know why, but that favor will come in handy for us, mark my words."

I liked that she'd said "us."

Tuesday sat up straighter in her seat and said loudly, "Who wants to play Truth or Dare?"

Russell's hand shot up in the air.

"Let's do it," Trevor said.

"As long as I don't have to eat anything disgusting, I'll play," Holly said.

"That's what Truth is for, doy," Kris scoffed.

"Don't be a witch," Holly snapped. "I'm just saying I'm not about to, like, eat sequins and dog hair, okay? Sue me!"

"Here we go," Trevor said, slumping down in the seat and *still* sitting taller than me. "Russell, will you switch me places and sit between the sisters?"

"Yeah, no way, I'm stayin' where I am," Russell said with a chuckle. "The junior high kids are chill."

Tuesday looked at me expectantly, like she was hoping for me to play. She smiled warmly, and I thought for the gazillionth time how rad it would be to have her as a real friend, not just a castmate.

"Count me in."

Later, when everyone else was sleeping, Russell nudged me with his hairy knee. I looked up at him, and he pushed his naturally curly hair out of his eyes to meet my gaze.

"Hey, Stevie, I just wanted to, like, say sorry about . . . you know . . . what, like, happened with DeLeon," Russell said, scratching the stubble on his chin. "I've been there." He laughed a little.

"Casey Kasem spilled your secrets on national radio?" I asked, making a joke of it, feeling less jokey on the inside.

"Not exactly like that," he said. "But I *did* use spray snow to write a message to a girl on the street in front of her house, asking her to the Homecoming dance."

"I take it she said no," I said empathetically.

"For sure." He made a clicking sound with his mouth.

"Sorry." I sighed. "At least spray snow washes right off."

"Unless you mistake it for paint and pour turpentine on it," Russell said. "That's, like, exactly what the girl's dad did, so my message stayed in the middle of her street for six months."

"Oh man," I groaned.

"Yeah, well." Russell shrugged. He was quiet for a few seconds, thinking. "Even so, I'm, like, glad I went for it. It's worse

not ever trying." He kneed me again softly. "It's brave, doing that. You're brave."

"You are too, Russell," I said.

"Yeah, well," he said, smiling shyly before putting his headphones back on.

I smiled, too.

29.

THE STRANGEST PLACE we spent the night on tour was a high school in Alabama.

Longleaf looked like a normal high school—but it was a *high school*, not a hotel or host family's house or campground or even a community center. People didn't sleep in high schools! But according to Margo, apparently, the kids of Synchronicity did.

"This reminds me of a ghost story I heard once," Kris said as us kids from the van followed the rest of the cast and chaperones down the wide main hallway of the school, long gray lockers lining one side, dimming summer light casting shadows through the windows on the opposite wall.

Tuesday and I were in the center of our van mob, flanked by

the older kids. It felt like we'd become a pod of our own, riding together, daring one another to smell armpits and say the alphabet backward. The way Russell had eyed Joey when we'd arrived, I wondered if he'd gotten a little protective of me.

"I remember that one," Holly agreed with her sister. "The PE teacher?"

"Totally," Kris said, their conversation lost to everyone else. "With the thing. And the—"

"I *know*," Holly answered, and they both laughed, reminding me that they shared a special twin language that Wes had given up trying to speak.

Think of the devil, Wes hung back like a boulder in a river until Tuesday and I were on either side of him. He started talking a mile a minute, like he'd been saving up his words for seven hours straight.

"Hey, you guys, we should go explore after we get our sleeping bags set up in the gym. Maybe there are some gymnastics mats we can use for padding. Otherwise, the floor's gonna be mega hard. Anyway, about exploring, I heard my mom telling the other chaperones there are cots in the nurse's room. That's where they're sleeping. They're just gonna make the older kids be in charge and probably smoke and play poker in the teachers' lounge."

"I've got an even better idea," Tuesday said deviously.

Wes looked intrigued, but Tuesday didn't tell us what she was thinking until after the school principal and the adults had

disappeared, leaving twenty-six kids alone in a strange high school gymnasium.

That's when Tuesday revealed her idea.

It was a kind of hybrid between a scavenger hunt and Truth or Dare—but without any Truth option—where small teams had to sneak through the school and find as much cool junk as possible before time ran out. Everyone would meet back in the gym and compare items; the team with the best loot won.

Twenty kids agreed to play, so Tuesday said there would be five teams of four.

"Who wants to be team captains?" Tuesday called. A handful of arms shot up, including Joey's. "Okay, how about Josh, Brandon—and . . . uh . . . Holly . . . and . . . Kimberly." She frowned just slightly before adding, "And Joey." She gestured to the line through the center of the basketball court. "Captains line up there. Everyone else go over there"—she motioned to one end of the court—"and they'll take turns picking."

"Who goes first?" Brandon asked, looking very serious about the rules.

"Oldest to youngest?" Tuesday asked with a shrug.

Everyone agreed, and Holly, the oldest by a couple of months, went first.

"I choose Russell," she said confidently, looking like she was playing to win. A bunch of people groaned because Russell was the most athletic—and tall enough to reach up-high treasures easily.

"I'm next?" Kimberly asked, looking around. After getting a bunch of nods and thumbs-ups, she said sweetly, "Courtney."

Joey jumped ahead even though it was Brandon's turn. He folded his arms over his muscular chest and slowly scanned the remaining thirteen options. I felt my cheeks warm when his eyes darted by me. Of course he was going to pick Shane; I wished he'd just get on with it. But then, he said, "Christy."

If there was one thing I was glad about, it was that I wouldn't be on Christy's team. It wasn't her fault that Joey had kissed her, but I still didn't want to talk to her—and I definitely didn't want to be on a team with both of them.

Christy looked a little uncomfortable as she went to stand by Joey.

"Go already, Brandon!" Tuesday said, breaking the silence.

He hesitated for a few seconds, probably trying to decide who would be most likely to help him win. In games and sports, Brandon was competitive. But then he surprised me.

"Stephanie Bea Finnegan," he proclaimed in a British accent.

I couldn't help but laugh at his booming voice and beaming smile as I walked over to join him. I wasn't chosen last, and more important, no matter what, ultimately, my brother had my back.

The selections circled around, and every time it was our turn to call someone, Brandon did it in a different accent. It was more fun than Tuesday's actual game, which turned out to be a flop. But before the game, after Brandon had just called "Robyn

Elizabeth Rose" in the worst Australian accent I'd ever heard, I noticed Joey watching me while I was in mid-belly laugh.

Surprisingly, his gaze didn't derail me. I just turned around in my white top and striped shorts and helped my brother decide which accent to do next.

It felt good to be the one to turn away first.

MOST OF THE classroom and office doors in the school were locked, so no one could really get anything good, but it was cool to wander around in a deserted high school for a while. When we all made it back to the gym, people were still in a game-playing mood. The dares started up again . . .

I dare you to put on makeup with your eyes closed.

I dare you to jump off the side of those bleachers.

I dare you to let me pummel you with volleyballs for thirty seconds.

I dare you to skip backward across the basketball court for the entire duration of "We Built This City."

Robert Sandoval, cousin to Little Josh, said, "Joshie, I dare you to jump in the pool fully clothed."

"Easy, point me to the pool," Josh said without hesitation, puffing up his chest to make himself look cool, stretching his massive frame, his icy eyes sparkling with adventure.

"It's that way." Robert pointed toward the back of the school.

Through the gym windows, we could see the darkened track around a football field and, off to the right side, a sleepy pool surrounded by a chest-high fence.

"I can just step over that thing," Josh said, sounding cocky.

"The parentals will see you," Kris said to Josh, matter-of-fact.

"That's the *challenge*," Robert said. "Jumping in a pool is easy. Jumping in a pool without being seen by the chaperones, that's harder. Especially when you're an ogre like Joshie."

Josh put Robert in a headlock long enough to ruffle his hair, then released him. Robert ran his fingers through his mullet and, when he was satisfied that he looked okay, went on talking. "The nurse's office is that direction. The windows probably look right out at the pool."

"No problem," Josh said, stretching his arms overhead before turning toward the back door. He made it there in, like, three strides. Pressing into the bar to unlock the door, he said, "Let me back in when I knock. I'm not sleeping outside."

"Oh my god, he's going to do it!" Kimberly said.

"Let's watch!" Courtney said, rushing over to the windows.

In a matter of seconds, every cast member was crowded around the dirty panes, struggling to see through the dark. There were a few lights surrounding the field but none near the pool area.

"This would make a great Stephen King setting," Amy said quietly. "Add some fog, and Josh is toast."

Next to her, Tuesday lost it laughing. "You're seriously horror-obsessed, you know that, right?"

Amy tossed her hair off her right shoulder. "And proud of it."

They were shushed by several kids as everyone watched Little Josh sprint from tree to tree, pausing for a few seconds between moves. He disappeared against the wall of the building.

"Hey—"

"Where'd he go?"

"No fair!"

"He's an ignoramus."

"No, he's being smart—"

"There he is!"

"Where?"

"Right there! He made it!"

Josh stepped up to the fence and easily vaulted over. Around the side of the brick pool house, he vanished for a minute. We waited, nobody saying a word. Then he reappeared again.

"He's really going to do it," Joey said.

"Not if our mom looks outside," Holly said. "Then Little Josh is gonna be in big trouble."

I blinked, eyes wide, scanning for chaperones, annoyed at myself for knowing that Joey was exactly three people to my left. I wanted to quit thinking about him!

We all watched as Josh rounded the pool like a tiger stalking its prey, seeming like he was trying to figure something out. He crouched down and pulled at something at one end, then walked to the other and repeated the move.

"What's he doing?" Tuesday asked.

"It must have a pool cover," Brandon said. "He's probably trying to figure out how to get it off, which can be complicated depending on which type of cover it is." No one asked how he knew, but he added, "I was a junior lifeguard."

"Yeah, yeah, we know," Kris muttered.

Everyone started talking over one another about how to remove a pool cover—who knew and who didn't—just as Little Josh threw up his hands in a shrug and jumped on top of the pool cover itself.

A few people laughed at first, when we could still see Little Josh. But then he sank like he was on quicksand. We saw his arms flailing, and then he disappeared.

"That doesn't look good," Wes said.

"He's tangled in the cover!" Robert yelled. "He's going to drown! He's a crap swimmer!"

"Why did you dare him to jump in a pool, then?" Holly screamed at Robert.

Brandon and I looked at each other and, without word or thought, sprinted together toward the exit, commotion exploding behind us.

Bursting through the door, we didn't try to hide in the shadows, we cut diagonally through the grass—the straightest path to Josh. I couldn't hear any splashing or cries for help, but then again, my heart was pounding so hard I could barely hear anything else at all.

Brandon reached the fence two seconds before I did. He clasped his hands and held them out, and like we'd choreographed it, I stepped up, up, and over, my feet tingling with the landing against the concrete deck on the other side. Brandon quickly followed.

"It's loose on that side," Brandon said, pointing to the far corner. "Loosen the rest to get the cover off. I'll go in."

I moved before he stopped talking, racing to untie the cover straps where they were knotted to metal loops in the concrete, thanking my lucky stars I'd helped remove pool covers many times before swim meets. As soon as I exposed a section of pool for him to go through, not having a clue exactly where Josh was, Brandon dove in, fully clothed.

"Crap, crap, crap, crap, crap," I whispered to myself as I went from knot to knot, untying and pulling, inch by inch. If I didn't get the cover under control, Brandon could easily get trapped, too!

I was aware of other voices, but they sounded far away, except then Wes was right next to me, and more kids appeared. They followed my lead, untying straps on the deep-end side of the pool, working together to heave the cover off.

We'd exposed half of the pool when Brandon reappeared with Josh under his arm. When they surfaced, Josh sputtered and puked up pool, then sputtered some more. We all watched as Brandon held him near the side of the pool until Josh could hold on himself.

He was okay.

"Holy crap," I said to Wes.

"You can say that again." He wiped his forehead.

"Dude, you, like, saved my life," Josh said to Brandon.

"Thank my sister, too," Brandon said. "We'd probably both have drowned if Stevie weren't here."

"The Finnegans are lifesavers!" Josh said. "And I win the dare!"

Everyone started yelling at Josh for scaring them to death, especially Robert, then someone pushed someone in the pool, and someone else did, too, and soon we were all in the dark water with our clothes on, laughing our faces off, happy that all of us were still alive.

The chaperones never came out or found out about Josh.

They weren't even there.

While we'd been sneaking around the school trying to avoid them, worried they'd show up and ruin our fun, they'd gone to downtown Mobile to go dancing without telling anyone. I guess they assumed the threat of them would be enough to keep us on our best behavior.

30.

I DIDN'T SLEEP at all that night at Longleaf High. A bunch of kids snored, but being in the same room as Joey was giving me emotional hives. It didn't matter that the room was a basketball court, and Joey and I were so far apart we'd be on opposing teams. The noisiness of his silence hurt my ears.

I checked the time on my white, pink, and blue Swatch, stepped over Wes's sleep-smiling self, then tiptoed outside, careful not to wake anyone. I held my breath while inching the door open and closed again. Then I walked barefoot through the dewy grass, inhaling the freshness of the morning, already warm as afternoon, scaling the fence of the pool—awkwardly without my brother's help, glad no one was there to see me get stuck momentarily at the top.

In my Mickey Mouse muumuu, I sat down next to the diving board at the deep end of the still-half-uncovered pool and dropped my feet into the water. The sun was just coming up, and the sky was on fire, reds and oranges reflecting off the surface of the peaceful water.

I spaced out, thinking that Mobile, or what I'd seen of it, was beautiful, when I heard someone else jump over the fence.

"Hey, Stevie," Christy said softly, like she was afraid she'd wake up the day. "Can't sleep?"

I shrugged. "Obviously." I didn't mean it to sound rude, but maybe it did. Christy didn't seem to notice, though.

"Me neither," she said, sitting down, dunking her feet. I watched her pink toenails sink. "That was intense earlier with Josh, huh?"

I glanced at her and away. "Yeah, it was."

I wished she'd leave, and wishing she'd leave made me feel horrible because up until Joey had planted *my* kiss on *her* cheek, Christy had been one of my idols. He'd ruined it!

"It's really lucky that you and Brandon knew what to do," she said. "I don't know what would have happened if you guys weren't here."

"Huh." I didn't know what else to say.

We swished our feet in the water and watched the sunrise for a few minutes in silence. Then she changed the subject to something I did *not* want to talk about.

"I'm sorry about what happened with Joey." Her voice was so caring it almost sounded like we were friends.

"It's not surprising he picked you over me," I muttered.

Christy sucked in her breath. "What are you talking about?"

I rolled my eyes but didn't look at her even though I could feel her piercing stare. "What are *you* talking about?" I sounded like a major jerk, and I didn't even care.

"Stevie, I mean the dedication," she explained. "I didn't think Joey's reaction was all that copacetic."

"I don't need a refresher; I was there," I said, eyes on the droopy trees surrounding the property. They reminded me of something that should be on the cover of a storybook. "It's obvious why he reacted that way," I added, rolling my eyes again. She didn't say anything, so I spelled it out. "He likes *you*. He kissed *you*." Saying it out loud to Christy made tears spring to my eyes. I covered my face with my palms. "I'm, like, so embarrassed I could die. And he hasn't even mentioned it, but, like, everyone's always looking at me. And you're, like, the coolest person on Earth, so of *course* he likes you and not me!"

"Stevie!" Christy said, worried. She pulled on my wrist and leaned over so I'd have to look at her. "Listen to me. I don't like Joey DeLeon. I don't know what he was thinking, but I definitely did *not* want him to kiss me. It's not like he asked me for permission, because if he had, I would have said no."

Still with one hand over my right eye like a makeshift pirate, I sniffed and asked, "Really?" Then, "Why not?"

Christy sighed. "Because he's not my type. He's not . . . I like someone else."

"Who?" I couldn't help but ask, finally dropping my other hand and looking into Christy's eyes, which were so blue they outshone the pool.

She hesitated, like she was thinking of telling me, then shook her head. "It's not important. I think I'm in the same boat as you." I must have looked confused. "I like someone, but I don't think they like me back."

"I don't know how that's possible." I swished my toes back and forth again, and she mimicked my movements, her feet deeper because her legs were longer.

"Believe me, it is," she said sadly. "Anyway, I wish you would have told me about Joey . . . like, that you liked him. Like when we stayed together?"

"Why would it matter?" I leaned over and rescued a bee, cupping my hand under it and setting it gently on the concrete next to me. The bee shook its wings dry and flew away.

She looked at me seriously. "I would have warned you. You're too good for him anyway." I tsked. "No, seriously. You're the kind of person who saves bees and people—like Little Josh. You're polite to host families, and don't think I haven't noticed when you've put my costumes away, Stevie Finnegan." I turned bright red as she said, "You're a helper. And Joey's . . . he's kind of rude sometimes. And . . . he's a flirt who just kind of wants all the girls to like him. Like it's a game to him or something."

"I don't know about that."

"I do," she said, running her fingertips through the water.

"I'm not the first girl he's tried to kiss this tour."

My posture caved in like a house hit by a tornado. And then, without thinking much about it, I tipped forward into the water. Bubbles flittered around my head as I shouted out my frustration, my eyes open and stinging in the chlorinated water.

When I came up, Christy was frowning at me. "I hope you meant to do that."

I nodded. "Pools are my happy place."

She smiled a little. "That's like singing for me."

"Sing something," I said boldly, treading water in my Mickey Mouse nightshirt.

"What, like, right now?" she asked warily.

"Sure," I said. "We're both feeling sad about liking people who don't like us. The water is making me feel better. You need to sing."

She titled her head to the side. "I don't really sing around people."

"I would never make you feel bad." My feet flapped back and forth like flippers.

Christy hesitated, then said, "You know what, Stevie, I don't think you ever would. You're a good friend."

"We're *friends*?" I asked.

She laughed. "Well . . . yeah! What else would you call us?"

"Castmates?" I asked, feeling ridiculous.

"Nah, we've bonded over crushes now," she said, tightening her ponytail like she did before shows. "That makes us real friends."

I smiled at her as she stood up and walked to the diving board, climbing up like it was a stage. I swam out to the center of the pool until I was in front of her. When she got to the edge of the diving board, standing in her bare feet and pink flower pajamas, she looked at me seriously. "Our secret, right?"

I nodded and said, "Pinkie swear."

Looking off into the distance, cutting through the quiet morning, Christy sang—quietly at first.

"We built this city."

She cleared her throat, then took a deep breath. "I'm starting over," she said.

I gave her a thumbs-up. She took another breath, and just when I thought she was going to chicken out, she sang for real.

"We built this city."

Oh.

Chills raced up my spine, fueled by the power in her voice.

"We built this city."

I hadn't even heard what she could do yet. She lifted her chin a little more and belted out:

"We built this city on rock and roooOOOOLL!"

Christy held on to the last note for so long I thought her voice would crack, but it didn't. The sound rocketed away from the pool and across the football field toward the storybook trees and the blue sky beyond. It turned my arms to gooseflesh; I shivered in the pool. I'd never heard anyone sing like that; I couldn't believe she had that in her.

She didn't sing the rest; she just smiled bashfully as I cheered, an audience of one wearing pajamas in a swimming pool. She sat down on the board and I floated closer to her, and after I asked her a billion questions about singing and she asked me a billion questions about swimming, we made our way inside, me wringing out my shirt as we tiptoed together across the grass.

It would have been a good start to the day, except when we made it back, everyone was awake, and the situation seemed tense. Margo had pulled Brandon aside and was lecturing him with her whole body, arms flailing, lips moving, head tilting, weight shifting. She looked mad.

I thought it was about Little Josh nearly drowning at first, even though that didn't make much sense, since Brandon had *saved* him.

"Come with me," Margo said loudly, taking off toward the doors to the hallway.

Brandon followed her, and I wanted to ask him what was going on, but his attention wasn't directed at me—he was looking at Joey. And not in a nice way.

"Thanks a lot, DeLeon," Brandon said harshly.

Joey threw up question hands. "What'd I do?"

"As if you don't know," Brandon snapped back.

And then I got it. Joey had told Margo about Brandon's seizure. Clenching my jaw, I wondered if Joey had done it to get back at me for embarrassing him in front of everyone by making life miserable for Brandon.

Now Margo was going to make Brandon call home, and then maybe he'd have to *go* home. And it probably meant he wouldn't get to play football next year. Even though I'd worried about that possibility, it made me sad to see his hopes dashed.

After the gym doors slammed shut, I looked back at Joey. He was telling Shane and Kimberly a story, standing closer to Kimberly. *Close* to Kimberly. He didn't even care what was about to happen to Brandon, and it seemed he'd moved on to flirting with someone new already.

Jerk.

31.

ALL I KNEW was my brother was allowed to stay, but he had to room with the chaperones, which put him in a rightfully rank mood. And Joey the secret-spilling, embarrassed-about-dedications, Christy-and-whoever-else-kissing jerk just went on with his life.

Gah!

In Dallas, Texas, after we performed at a community theater, we were told that an older couple with a lot of space had signed up to host seven of us girls that night. I was elated to hear I'd be staying with Tuesday, Amy, and Christy in addition to Holly, Courtney, and Kris.

"Ask Tuesday what her favorite color is," Wes whispered before

we parted ways. "And ask her what type of dates she likes to go on. And her favorite flower. But don't tell her I told you to ask."

"She'll know," I said, rolling my eyes. "If I suddenly go, 'Hey, Tuesday, do you like carnations?' she's totally going to know you put me up to it."

"Okay, fine, don't ask that stuff, but swear you'll tell me everything new you learn about her," Wes said seriously. "I don't want to mess this up."

"You won't," I said, patting him on the shoulder. "Really, Wes. You can chill. You're awesome."

Wes looked at Joey, goofing around by the double glass doors with Shane, as usual, then back at me with eyes that meant business. "You're awesome, too, Stevie. Never forget it."

Our host family, Mr. and Mrs. McGill, managed a ranch with a guesthouse on the property—the guesthouse was bigger than my normal house at home. The couple fed us barbecue for dinner around a campfire across from a horse corral; the cows were out somewhere roaming acres of land, and we could hear them mooing softly in the distance.

Mr. and Mrs. McGill asked about each one of us, listening when we talked like they wanted to remember.

Everyone started off telling them about surface things, like their favorite subjects in school, but something about the moment

and the McGills' earnestness made people start sharing for real.

Courtney revealed that she'd scored just as high as her sister, Robyn, on the PSAT but that for some reason, their parents only told people how well Robyn had done.

"Parents are tough," Tuesday said. "I'd love to stop skating competitively, but I don't want to disappoint mine."

"My dad doesn't know I love to sing," Christy said, looking right at me when she said it, me nodding in support.

"My mom doesn't know I have a boyfriend," Holly admitted.

"My mom doesn't know how much time I spend in the library," Kris said.

"My parents don't know I want to go to China and meet my birth parents," Amy chimed in. "I think my mom's afraid I'm not going to love her anymore. Or that my plane will crash. Or that I'll read too many horror novels on the way and break my brain."

Everyone laughed as I tried to think of something to say. My parents were pretty cool, I didn't have any secret skills or dreams, I *definitely* didn't have a secret boyfriend, and after the Dedication debacle, I was an open book. Well, except . . .

"I've never been invited to a sleepover," I blurted out. "Or to anyone's birthday party." Wes didn't like parties. "Or to a friend's house other than Wes's."

I looked down at my hands.

"My birthday's next month, and you're definitely invited," Christy said.

"You're invited to mine, too," Courtney said.

"Same," Kris said, "duh."

"Sounds like your social calendar is about to change, young lady," Mr. McGill said.

We toasted marshmallows, and then, when the mosquitos started eating us alive, the McGills shooed us off to the guesthouse to "kick off your boots and settle in."

None of us had on boots, of course, because that would have been super weird.

The guesthouse was a huge log cabin with a plush plaid couch; massive, comfy chairs; and the type of oiled-wood furniture that any parent would yell, "Coaster!" if you went near it with a beverage. We dropped our sleeping bags and duffels in the bunk room and went back to the family room to hang out.

Turns out it was like a giant sleepover—my first one—and it was amazing. Christy had declared us friends, and it felt like Tuesday and I were, too. I was used to Amy's mile-a-minute monotone and wasn't surprised when she made us all look for a Ouija board. (Thankfully, no one found one.)

Holly sweetly painted everyone's fingernails neon orange—except Kris's—and Kris *really* wanted to do crank calls, but there wasn't a phone in the guesthouse. Courtney taught me how to do a tough dance part in "9 to 5" and thanked me for covering for her when she was puking in Atlanta.

Holly crouched next to the TV in the living room, slowly changing the channel, trying to find MTV.

"This is so killer!" Tuesday said, gathering the hem of her

humongous T-shirt and starting to tie it into a knot at her hip. "I hope they show 'Power of Love.' Robyn said it has scenes from *Back to the Future* in it!"

"There!" Kris shouted at the top of her lungs, making me jump. "You've got it!"

The animation for the MTV Countdown was almost over. Everyone started *shhh*ing one another as loudly as they could.

Martha Quinn with her awesome style and mismatched earrings introduced the video for "Shout" by Tears for Fears. "Would I Lie to You?" by Eurythmics came on next, and several girls got up and danced.

"Want me to braid your hair?" Christy asked, scooting over on the couch so she was right behind me. "I'm really good at it."

"Sure," I said, as if I'd pass up that offer.

She divided my hair into three sections and combed through it with her fingers, then started weaving it together, right over center, left over center, right over center . . .

"Hey, Christy?"

"Yeah?"

"Will you really teach me some sign language sometime? I mean, like, if you're not super busy after school starts."

"Totally!" she said easily. "We can pick a day and meet up at my house." Her finger snagged on a small knot in my hair. "Sorry."

"Didn't hurt," I said. In fact, the motion of her delicate fingers moving through my hair was calming me practically to the

point of drooling. But she woke me up with her next question.

"Are you doing okay? Has Joey, like, said anything?"

She'd said it quietly, but the show had paused for a commercial break, and Tuesday, Amy, and Holly turned toward me. Courtney, sitting sideways in one of the enormous chairs, feet dangling over the arm, looked up from her *Seventeen* magazine. Kris hurried out of the kitchen with a huge green plastic bowl of popcorn. It seemed they all wanted to know, too.

Christy finished the braid and wound a scrunchie around it, then scooted over and patted the couch next to her. I climbed up, sitting cross-legged.

"Spill it," Kris commanded.

"I'm okay," I said. "I'm embarrassed, but, like, okay."

"You have nothing to be embarrassed about," Kris said, popping a kernel into her mouth. "It was rad. Anyone normal would be flattered. Joey is from Mars. How many letters did you send?"

"Seventeen," I admitted. Kris laughed, but I didn't feel bad about it.

"That's determination," Tuesday said.

"The same song every time?" Courtney asked curiously.

"No, not all the time. I mixed it up."

"I'm sorry he wasn't cool about it," Tuesday said. Christy nudged me with her knee, probably silently saying she was sorry, too.

"I asked a guy to Sadie Hawkins in the cafeteria in front of the entire school, and he rejected me," Holly said. We all looked at her in surprise.

"That guy was, like . . . gag me!" Kris said in solidarity.

"I wrote my number in my crush's yearbook on the last day of school, and he never called," Christy said.

"I was dumped right before tour," Kris said, laughing it off.

"I got dumped last year on my birthday," Courtney chimed in.

We all groaned, and everyone agreed that heartbreak was the worst. "The thing that bothers me the most is that Joey still hasn't said anything to me about it," I admitted. "And . . ." I hesitated for a second before sharing the next thing, careful because I didn't know how much Brandon had told our castmates about why he had gotten a Margo talking-to. "Joey and I had a secret, and it was about Brandon . . ." Christy's eyes snapped to mine. "And Joey told, and I think he only did it because he was mad at me. Like revenge or something."

"What was the secret?" Christy asked quietly.

I looked around. "Uh . . . um. I don't . . ."

"That's okay," she said. "I didn't mean to pry."

"No prob," I said, before refocusing on Joey. "It just sucks because he hasn't said, like, a *word*. I mean it's, like, fine to not like me back, but . . ."

"That's right!" Tuesday blurted out. "It's not fine to avoid you!"

"It's so immature," Courtney said, eyes back on her magazine now.

"Not after you sent seventeen song dedications," Kris said.

"The least he could do is acknowledge you. Boys are idiots."

"Not all boys," Tuesday said dreamily, smiling at me.

"He's too busy trying to impress *Shane* of all people," Amy said. The others laughed.

It felt weird, them saying bad stuff about Joey, and even Shane. I didn't like when people talked about other people behind their backs. "Let's not talk about this anymore," I said. "I just want to move on."

"Okay, but can I give you one piece of advice?" Courtney asked, looking up from her magazine again. I nodded. "You said you're sad Joey hasn't brought it up with you. Where's the rule that says *you* can't bring it up with *him*? This is the eighties, Stevie. If you want to talk to him, talk to him."

I hadn't thought of that.

"Maybe I will," I said, sitting up straighter on the couch. "Maybe I'll talk to him tomorrow! I'll confront him about spilling the secret, too!"

"Go for it!" Courtney said.

"Go, Stevie!" Tuesday said, clapping.

Christy was nodding and smiling at me, but she had sort of a strange expression on her face. I decided to ask her about it later because "Invincible" by Pat Benatar came on MTV—the song that'd played right before the dedication in Orlando. The song that had made me feel like I had fire in my veins. And it did again in Dallas.

I leapt off the couch and started dancing with the others.

"Nice moves!" Holly said over the music.

I shrugged.

"She's always first to get the choreography!" Tuesday said loudly.

I shrugged again.

"You should come with me to my jazz dance class!" Amy said, copying a step I was doing so we were moving in sync.

"Maybe I will!" I said again, my mantra for the evening. Maybe I will talk to Joey. Maybe I will take up dancing. Maybe I will become a girl with friends and confidence and that star sparkle, on and off the stage. Maybe I will—

I gasped and flipped around. "Courtney! Write down the lyrics!"

Courtney already had a pen nearby for the quiz in the magazine. She grabbed it and did as I said, unquestioning, scribbling across the cover model's face.

"We can all work out the choreography!"

"What's going on?" Amy asked, her hypercolor sweatshirt changing with the heat of her dancing. "I don't get what we're doing."

Tuesday laughed and said, "I don't know for sure, either, but it seems like we're learning a new number for the show."

We stayed up late into the night. Miracle of miracles, Holly had "Invincible" on one of her mixtapes, and the guesthouse had

a stereo, so we rewound and played and rewound and played until Courtney had the lyrics. Then Christy bashfully said she had a suggestion.

It tumbled out of her. "Like, we don't have to at all, but would you guys be okay with, like, signing the chorus? Just like the *invincible* part? Except I think we'd have to sign *unbeatable*. Anyway, it's a cool sign and it would be rad because my parents could understand."

"Totally," several of us said in unison.

"What's it look like?" I asked, wiping sweat off my forehead. Little pieces of my braid had fallen out and were stuck to my face.

Christy put her left arm horizontal like it was lying on a table, palm flat. She put her right elbow on top of her left hand, that palm flat at first, too, but then she squished it into a fist. It looked like a rad dance move but meant something so much more. I loved it.

"That's perfect!" I squealed. "Teach us the rest!"

After we went through the signs a few times, we worked more on the choreography. It wasn't that hard, since we were all used to picking up choreo quickly. We all took turns making up pieces of the dance until it was done.

I looked around at my bunkmates, feeling supported—like I had real friends. And their enthusiasm was contagious. Amy, who was normally reserved, was shouting over everyone. Tuesday's larger-than-life energy radiated out of her like when Mario gets

a star. I'd never seen Kris smile so broadly, or Courtney, who normally acted all mature like a grown-up, laugh so hard she snorted. Polite Holly burped her soda and bossed us all around to get the choreo right. Christy, normally the star, cheered everyone else on.

Watching them, I knew I needed nights like this, friends like these, maybe more than a hand to hold during a couples' skate.

I wanted that, too, someday. But tonight, this was perfect.

32.

OUR PERFORMANCE THE next day was at a mall in Dallas.

Margo made us arrive early and rehearse because she said we had all missed marks the last few performances. Plus, she was concerned about numbers like "Magic" and "Eye of the Tiger" on the slippery, freshly polished tile.

We weren't allowed to turn on the music until showtime since the mall was already open. Moms with shopping bags hanging off the handles of their babies' strollers and teens wanting to kill time in an air-conditioned anywhere went by as we awkwardly and unenthusiastically blocked our numbers like mimes.

"This is humiliating," Wes said under his breath as a group of giggling girls around our age passed by. We weren't on a stage, only an open space in front of Sears. "We look like dorks."

"Finally, you understand the truth about yourself," said Kris as she danced by with Russell.

Joey had somehow managed to get Margo to switch up the partners, so I was dancing with Shane, and we were doing everything we could *not* to look at each other.

"How's it going, Stevie?" Russell asked, eyeing Shane.

I opened my mouth to answer but was silenced by Margo. "Stop talking or we'll do it again!" she yelled, her voice echoing throughout the cavernous space and attracting any attention that wasn't already on us. Several kids groaned . . . very, very quietly.

After we made it through "Summer Nights," Wes and I rushed toward seats off to the side, partially hidden by a huge fake plant with dusty leaves. We watched the torture continue for others; it was probably the only time I was glad not to be performing "Magic."

"Ready?" Margo shouted to the skaters, not caring who heard. Margo didn't seem flustered by anything. Her son, on the other hand, was dying of embarrassment next to me as he sank deeper into his folding chair. I worried it might fold him in.

"Hold on!" Kris shouted back at her mom, sounding more like Margo than I'd ever realized. "I need to re-lace my skate!"

Margo sighed, muttering to Ms. Freeman, Mr. Schneider, and the Johnsons, the adults laughing about whatever she said.

"Hey," I whispered, "I have two secrets."

"Tell me," Wes said, still smashed low. He had on his royal-blue headband today; it was one of my favorites.

I held up my pointer finger. "Number one: I'm going to just go talk to Joey after our show." I lifted my chin. "I'm not waiting around for him to decide to talk to me."

"About time." Wes smiled. "I'm glad. What's the other secret?"

I put two fingers up. "Number two: You'll find out at our last performance. It's going to be awesome."

"THIS IS YOUR chance," Tuesday whispered, with Christy nodding encouragingly, in the mall hallway that'd served as a dressing room during the performance. "A bunch of them are at the arcade, including Joey."

I swallowed hard, sure I looked like a cartoon character with a visible lump in my throat. I'd never been more nervous about anything in my life.

"You can do it," Christy said. "You're invincible!"

"We're right behind you," Tuesday said—she meant it literally. She and Wes were planning to go with me, but I'd told everyone else to stay behind. I didn't need a humongous audience.

With Wes to my left and Tuesday to my right, I made my way through the mall, by a shoe store and a Fotomat and a record

store and a place you could get your ears pierced, not talking, only majorly freaking out.

I was about to turn around when I saw the rainbow arches of Time-Out. Before I had time to rethink it, I stepped from the serene mall into the dark, beeping, sweat-smelling arcade, which transported me back home, since all Time-Outs were the same.

The same house rules hung overhead in black, red, and yellow—NO SMOKING, NO FOOD OR BEVERAGES, NO GAMBLING, NO LOITERING. The guard near the door wore the same blue-and-black uniform; the manager near the back wore the same maroon blazer.

The sameness was comforting, making me feel like I *could* do it.

"Shane is a top scorer on *Frogger*—I bet he's there," I said.

"Yeah, but Joey likes *Galaga*," Wes said, adding, "the worst game ever."

He beamed when Tuesday said, "Totally!"

Ultimately, we found Joey and Little Josh waiting for a turn while Shane played *Flintstones* pinball. Brandon was nearby and looked intrigued when he saw us approaching, like he knew something was about to happen. He didn't stop playing his own pinball game, but he shifted his stance so his shoulders were facing slightly more in my direction.

"I'll meet you guys outside," I said to Wes and Tuesday.

Tuesday nodded and left, but Wes waited a few seconds, then leaned close and whispered, "Don't let him make you feel small."

He looked at me with his intense stare that sometimes felt like he could see my feelings, then turned away.

I summoned all the guts I had in the world and stepped closer to Joey, tapping him on the shoulder. He did a double take; his face hardened when he realized it was me.

"What's up, Stevie," he said flatly.

"Can I talk to you?" I asked quietly.

He glanced at Shane, who was still playing but now had a smirk on his face. "Yeah, what's up?" Joey asked. He blew a bubble, and it popped loudly before he sucked the gum back into his mouth. I could see I was going to be dealing with Niagara Falls flyswatter Joey here.

"Can we, like, walk over there for a sec?" I motioned toward the alcove by the entrance. "I'm sure Josh would save your spot in line."

"Yeah, I'm good here," Joey said, putting his hands in his shorts pockets and puffing up his chest a little. He checked with Shane again.

Josh was watching us intently. He scratched his chin where it looked like a zit was thinking about making an appearance and stepped away but didn't leave.

"So, like, what?" Joey asked, glancing at me, not even giving me the gift of eye contact. I'd never seen him just so plain rude. It made me feel sick. It made me feel uneasy. It made me feel . . .

Small.

Don't let him make you feel small.

"No," I said, standing as tall as I could, which was just a couple of inches shorter than Joey. I pushed my shoulders back and raised my chin an inch.

"No what?" Joey said with a laugh, glancing at me again, chewing his gum loudly. Quickly. Nervously?

I grabbed his wrist and turned around, pulling him behind me like a puppy that didn't want to walk in the rain. Out of the corner of my eye, I saw my brother chuckle. I think he knew that Joey was in trouble. And I knew that if I needed him, Brandon was right there.

"Dude!" Joey said when I dropped his wrist in the front alcove and spun toward him. "Look, Stevie, I don't know how to say this, but it's not gonna happ—"

"You're not in charge here, Joey." I cut him off, acid in my tone, fist on my popped hip. He raised his dark eyebrows in surprise and opened his mouth to say something else. "Shut up and listen," I snapped, then took a breath. "I don't care that you don't like me back." I looked at him pointedly while he avoided my gaze—choosing to focus on the psychedelic carpeting instead. "What I care about is that you haven't told me that to my face."

"I just did, but you talked over me," he muttered.

"I mean before," I said. "All you had to say was—"

"What, Stevie?" He cut me off this time, eyes on me now so I saw his look of helplessness. "What should I have said to, like, make it okay? You did that in front of *everyone*. Like, my grandma listens to Casey Kasem!"

That caught me off guard. "Your *grandma*?"

"What can I say, she's cool," he said with a small laugh. "But when I called home, she was all, 'Tell me about your nice new girlfriend, Stevie.' Like she just assumed. But I don't..."

He glanced over at the pinball machine; Shane and Josh were watching us from afar. "I hate feeling backed into a corner," he said, looking at me again. In a softer voice, he said, "I'm sorry, Stevie. You're a cool girl. But it's just not like that . . . for me . . . about you . . ."

"I get it," I said, holding up my hands so he'd stop saying words. "That's all I wanted." I took another deep breath. "Now, on to the next thing. Why did you tell Margo about Brandon's seizure?"

Joey took a step back. "What?" he asked, surprised. "I didn't!" I folded my arms over my chest and stared at him menacingly. He held up his hands in surrender. "I swear, Stevie, I swear on my dog's life. I didn't say a thing. If people know, it is *not* because of me."

He may have been a flirty jerk who cared way too much about impressing his best friend, but he *did* seem genuine.

"Really?" I asked.

"Really."

"Fine."

He looked over his shoulder, then back at me. "So that's, like . . . that's it? You wanted to hear I don't like you and accuse me of something I didn't do?" he asked with a laugh. "Girls are so weird."

"I just wanted an acknowledgment," I said quietly. "I wanted you to say . . . *something*." It was my turn to look down. "I sent so many letters about how rad you are. You could at least take that as a compliment and say—"

"Thanks."

"Yeah, that's what I mean," I said, eyes on him again.

"No, I'm actually saying it," he clarified. "Thanks, Stevie. I kinda thought . . . maybe . . . like, I had a feeling you might have felt that way, and maybe there was a second I, like, thought about . . . but, like, I never could have imagined how this would all go."

"Well, you know what Margo says . . ."

"Live life with jazz hands," we said in unison, chuckling softly.

"I'm sorry if I embarrassed you," I said. "I didn't think about that part of it, how you might feel super weird to have a dedication read on national radio." I paused, then added, "And I totally did *not* expect that your grandma would hear it."

Joey waved it off. "It's cool." He looked over at the pinball machine again. "I guess I'm up. Are we copacetic?"

"Yeah," I said, wishing he'd have apologized for acting so rude before, for treating me like a toe fungus, for any of it, really. But it was okay. The conversation had been enough.

"Later, Stevie," Joey said, turning away before I had a chance to say anything else to him.

I watched his walk change from normal to a saunter the closer he got to his friends; I watched him casually check his

appearance in the reflection of a broken *Pac-Man* machine and double over laughing with Shane when he reached the pinball machine.

It didn't bother me, though. I could see Joey now for real, for who he was and not who I wanted him to be, and I didn't feel sad anymore. I wasn't a human Magic 8 Ball, so I didn't know what was to come, but there in the arcade, I knew one thing for sure: Joey wasn't the couples' skate partner I wanted anymore, and he'd never be again.

33.

IN OKLAHOMA CITY, Oklahoma, we got ready to perform at a Methodist church that gave me déjà vu.

"Have we been here before?" I asked Christy.

"Nope," Christy said. "But I get why you think that. After a while, all the places we perform at start to look the same."

She and I were assigned to apply black nail polish on the corners of the star boxes where the black paint had rubbed off to reveal white underneath. The white would wreck the black light number, Margo told us.

"You won't look like you're floating," she'd said. "It'll take away some of the magic."

We were two stops from home, three days from my own bed, three sleeps from my mom's meat loaf and my dad's big laugh and Brandon and me being back under one roof all the time—and starting the new school year with a bunch of new friends.

Except something was still bugging me.

"Remember when Hall & Oates raced to Oklahoma City last winter?" Christy asked casually. She had her legs crossed like a pretzel in front of the biggest box; I was straddling the medium-sized one. "Hall won. No, wait, was it Oates?"

"I don't remember," I said. "I don't know which is which."

"What's your favorite Hall & Oates song?" she asked.

I shrugged. "I can't remember the names."

"What's happening right now?" she asked, holding her nail brush in midair. "You live for pop music, and you can't think of the name of a Hall & Oates song?" She laughed at my blank stare. "Okaaaay . . . let's talk about something else. Holly told me she worked everything out with Margo so we can do our number at the last performance."

"Hmm," I said, eyes on my work. I leaned forward and blew lightly on what I'd just painted. She did the same.

"What's up?" she asked in a low tone.

"Nothing."

"There's no way that's true," she said. "You're practically zombified instead of geeking out with happiness about the awesome thing we're going to do . . . that *you* came up with!"

I didn't want to tell her I was still wondering who told Brandon's secret, because I thought she'd ask what the secret was.

I rolled my eyes and said, "I know, and I'm super psyched about it. But I'm also super freaked." The truth was that I didn't feel nervous about it at all. After confronting Joey, I felt, like the song said, invincible.

"Don't worry, Stevie."

"But what if I mess up?" I kept the ruse going.

"Stevie," Christy said seriously, in a low voice, looking at me with her deep blue eyes that reminded me of the Atlantic Ocean, "don't stop believing."

I looked at her curiously. "Did you just quote Journey at me?"

"You're just a small-town girl," she said, a sly smile on her face, "livin' in a lonely world."

"Stop," I said quietly, fighting a smile.

She quoted the next line.

"Christy!" I said, louder. Courtney, walking by, laughed at us.

Just then, Christy surprised me by belting out the chorus at the top of her lungs—in front of about five of our other castmates. A few of them joined in, because it was hard not to sing that song once someone had made it a total mutant earworm. Even Margo sang along.

"For real." Christy leaned in and said to me, the sound of badly sung lyrics over whatever was playing on the boom box in the background, "Everything's going to be copacetic."

And then, she did what she'd done the first day of tour. She put her pointer finger to her lips like she was saying *shhh*, but then made her hand flat and set it on her other hand, which was balled into a fist.

PROMISE.

I ACCIDENTALLY FOUND out the truth about Brandon's secret right before the show started that night.

Margo told me to go find Wes and Tuesday because it was time to get in makeup. I wandered outside and found them sitting on the church steps, only like an inch apart, holding hands. It was like I'd taken a time machine to the fifties: Tuesday was in her poodle skirt, and Wes had his hair slicked back and a deck of cards rolled in the sleeve of his white T-shirt, made to look like a pack of cigarettes.

I stopped short, feeling a strange mix of surprise and jealousy and giddiness all at the same time. I watched them for a few seconds, quietly talking to each other, Wes explaining why an elf was the best D&D character for her, and I wondered if my relationship with Wes was about to change. I wondered if we'd grow apart now that he had a girlfriend. That thought sat like a lemon after ice cream in my stomach, so I didn't dwell; I jogged down the steps.

"Yo," I said. "Margo wants us in makeup."

"It's hotter than the surface of the sun in there," Wes said. "It'll melt off." He patted the step next to him. "Cop a squat. We can tell her you couldn't find us."

"She's going to kill us." I shrugged and did as he'd said, careful not to smack him in the face with crinoline as I sat down.

"I'll take the blame."

"Our hero," Tuesday said jokingly. She leaned around Wes and looked at me. "Ready for our big surprise?"

I smiled and nodded. "For sure."

"Hey, that's not fair," Wes complained. "You guys can't bring up secrets in front of me if you're not going to tell me what they are."

"It's rad, I promise," I said.

"*So* rad," Tuesday agreed. "And it was all Stevie's idea."

Embarrassed, I changed the topic. "Speaking of secrets, it's driving me crazy that I don't know who ratted out Brandon about his . . . uh . . . secret." Tuesday had known about Brandon and football in the first place, but I didn't know what else she knew.

It was exhausting figuring out who knew what.

"Are you, like, talking about Brandon's epilepsy?" she asked, fiddling with one of her bracelets. I looked at Wes like, *Did you tell her that?* and he gave his head a sharp shake like, *No way, dude, I wouldn't.*

"How did you know?" I asked.

Tuesday looked at the sky like she was thinking. "Um, I think,

like, Brandon told me? A long time ago, like, maybe last year?"

Wes looked at her quickly. "Are you the one who told Margo he had a seizure on tour?"

"Nope," Tuesday said casually. "Is *that*, like, what you were talking about at the ranch, Stevie?"

"Yes!" I said. "But how did you know he had a seizure? Did Brandon tell you that, too?"

She shook her head, and the longer side of her hair hit her on the opposite cheek. "Amy told me. She was there, remember?" It was the host house with the doll room. Amy had been asleep when I'd gone back to the bedroom—but apparently, she hadn't been asleep all night.

"So then . . . who told Margo? That's what I'm trying to figure out. Because that person is going to be in big tr—"

"That was me."

Out of nowhere, Christy appeared beside me and sat down on the steps. "Margo sent me on a rescue mission. She *really* wants you guys in makeup—like, now."

I ignored the makeup thing. "You told the secret?" I asked, looking at her like she was speaking a foreign language. "You knew? And you told?"

"Yes," she said. "And yes, Tuesday told me, and yes, I told Margo." She looked genuinely worried. "I'm sorry. Are you mad?"

"Yes!" I said, but really, I was just confused. "Actually . . . I don't know. Does Brandon know you told?"

She shook her head, her long blond ponytail swishing with the movement. In her heavy stage makeup, she looked like she was in college.

"Then . . . Why shouldn't I be mad? Explain why you did it!" I was exasperated.

Wes loudly chewed his fingernail next to me, and I gave him a look. He pulled his finger out of his mouth. "Maybe we should just go in," he said.

"We should," Tuesday said, standing up and brushing off the back of her poodle skirt.

"Wait," I said, looking back at Christy. *"Why?"*

"I'm kind of like you," she said softly. "I try to do things for people I care about."

I didn't get it for a second—and then I did.

"Your crush is . . ." I swallowed hard. "My *brother*?"

She nodded, her head tilted to the side, blinking slowly like she was thinking of him. *Gross!* But also, maybe it was kind of cute?

"He's not the one who never called, is he?"

She smiled sadly and nodded again.

Christy had risked Brandon—and me—getting mad at her for doing something to protect him. Instead of being angry with her, I felt sad she knew how it felt to not have your feelings returned, that she did that kind gesture in secret. I was thankful someone else had been looking out for Brandon, too.

I leaned over and gave her a hug.

"You're not mad?" she asked into my shoulder.

"No way," I said.

"Are you going to tell him?"

"No way," I said again, and we both laughed a little. When I pulled out of the hug, Christy wiped away a tear. She must really like him.

That night during the performance, I finally noticed how often Christy looked at Brandon, how she hung on his words, how she positioned herself near him when she could. I thought they would have been great together, but you can't change how people feel about each other—and if he didn't like her back, there was nothing to be done.

Still, that night, I had a dream that the two of them got married at Casa Bonita in Denver, but instead of watching the cliff divers, they *were* the cliff divers. Then everyone ate warm sopaipillas with honey instead of wedding cake, and Christy became my sister-in-law.

It was weird, but that's how dreams work.

The point is, I wasn't mad at Christy, and even my dream knew that.

34.

OUR END-OF-TOUR CAST party happened after we brought down the house in Fort Collins, Colorado, which was only forty-five minutes from home.

Our last show, which was especially for our friends, families, neighbors, and teachers was tomorrow. Tonight, we were in the café at a roller rink, stuffing our faces with pepperoni pizza as Margo recounted stories of the tour like a stand-up comedienne, laughing as if we hadn't just lived through them, too. A storyteller forever, Margo poured lava over the memories and hardened them into legends.

When we were all stuffed to the gills, we hit the rink in pods. There were the oldest kids who wouldn't tour next year,

looking like grown-ups with their maturity and mustaches, too cool to skate, draped across two tables in a dark corner of the café.

There were the kids who alternated between trying to knock one another off their skates and acting chill and checking out the locals. Joey was in that group, admiring some girl he'd probably never see again after tonight as much as he admired his reflection in the full mirror every time he completed a loop.

There was Brandon, popping his collar, then missing a step but catching his balance, unaware that the coolest girl in the world was still looking out for him after he'd rejected her and would gladly help him up if he fell. There was Amy, skating backward effortlessly in a black unitard, her face neutral, but I knew she was having fun. There was Christy, laughing her head off about something Kris had said, pushing her pain somewhere else and living her life. There was Tuesday, in the middle of the rink, a jewelry box ballerina on wheels, twirling, twirling, twirling—until she spied Wes and me leaning on the carpeted wall.

My stomach flipped as she skated over, thinking she'd pull him away and leave me behind. Instead, she screeched to a halt between us and held out both hands, one for each of us to clasp.

Someone had requested "We Built This City," and it started right as our trio rolled onto the floor. Christy and Amy joined us, and we were a powerful five—the girls helping Wes manage to stay upright. Then, because it was our song, the theme song for the Synchronicity 1985 August tour, everyone came out, even the oldest kids, even the chaperones.

The deejay turned out the lights and spun the disco ball. We rolled in circles and sang our song as loudly as we could, most of us crying by the last note of the song.

Everyone was probably ready to go home and do normal life again.

That doesn't mean we weren't sad tour was ending.

35.

"MOMMY!" I SAID, running down the theater hallway toward the person I'd missed so much more than I'd realized. My mom dropped her purse two seconds before I nearly knocked her over in a hug. Margo had been a great stand-in this month, but there was nothing like my real mom.

"And I thought *you* were the one who was going to play football," she said to Brandon behind me, my mom still holding me tight.

"Huh? He told you?"

"He did," my mom said.

"I may be the football player," Brandon said confidently, "but she's pretty tough, too." He hesitated, then asked, "Did you make an appointment with Dr. Nelson?"

I felt my mom's nod. "Friday. Then we'll see."

"I want to do it." He sounded like he was forcing himself to be strong. "I want to live my life on my terms."

"If the doctor says it's okay, we'll support you." We were still wound up like a mall pretzel. "Hey, my little Stevie Bea," Mom said to me, stroking my hair. Tears came to my eyes. "I missed your face."

"I missed *your* face," I said, getting stage makeup all over her shoulder.

Finally, I stepped back. "Where's Dad?"

"Saving seats," Mom said. "I just couldn't wait to see my babies. You both look all grown-up."

Brandon rolled his eyes in embarrassment and checked to see if anyone else was around. Then he stepped in and kissed our mom on the cheek.

"We gotta go—the show's going to start," he said.

"I know, I know," Mom said, waving her hands. "I'll see you both after. Good luck."

She blew us dozens of kisses as we walked away. "Moms are weird," Brandon said.

"They're also awesome," I said. He half smiled. "Hey, Bran, can I look at your yearbook from last year?"

"Uh . . . why?" he asked, yanking open the heavy door that led to backstage and holding it for me.

"I just want to . . . like, um . . . get familiar with kids who will be at school." I smiled broadly so he wouldn't be able to see the lie coming out of my mouth.

He gave me a strange look, then said, "Sorry, I lost it."

"What do you mean you *lost* it?"

"Dude, I mean I lost it," he said. We were at the door to the dressing room. "There was an assembly, and I set it on the bleachers, and when I went back, it was gone. I've never even seen it myself."

"So you have no idea if anyone, like, wrote you a nice message or whatever?" I asked, matchmaking thoughts swirling in my head.

He rolled his eyes. "What, you mean, like, *never change*? I think I'll live without those."

Brandon walked over to where his costume bags were and started getting ready for our last performance. I had to push thoughts of him and Christy getting together out of my mind so I could focus, but they wouldn't be out of my head forever.

Maybe some weird dreams *did* come true after all.

36.

THIS WAS OUR stage.

We'd performed at the Civic Center in Cheyenne, Wyoming, so many times over the years that despite the fact that it took up an entire square city block and was one of the biggest buildings downtown; despite the totally humongous, multilevel auditorium; despite the bigger, brighter spotlights and booming sound; despite the daunting orchestra pit, which could seriously break an ankle if you fell into it, I wasn't tense at all—I could do the show in my sleep.

I was emotional, though. I got choked up the second Margo took the mic and began a speech about what an experience we'd all shared, and how much it'd meant to her and the other chaperones, and for a second, I wished we had a few more stops.

Margo's speech was pure cheese, but it was rad.

Next to her was a professional ASL interpreter for Christy's parents and their friends.

"I love these kids like my own," Margo said, tears in her eyes, her raspy voice ricocheting off the walls and high ceiling and back again. "They gave it their all this summer—they worked their butts off! I couldn't be prouder of the young women and men they've grown into." She wiped a tear that'd escaped; there were sniffles in the wings around me. "This is our last performance of the Synchronicity 1985 tour, and we're going to go out with a bang!"

We all hooted, and the audience clapped; when everything died down, Margo turned sideways, facing us instead of the audience. "I just want you kids to know that I'm so thankful for you. I consider myself lucky that I get to live in your sky, my shining stars."

Our parents, grandparents, aunts, uncles, cousins, neighbors, friends, and teachers cheered even louder than before.

Margo waved to the audience and left the stage, and we got into place for our last performance of "Summer Nights" this tour. The boppy beat began, and Trevor and Christy pretended like they were in love with each other, everyone else fake-singing backup about their fake fifties summer romance.

At the end of the song, my mom and dad stood up, cheering like maniacs. Brandon and I looked at each other and rolled our eyes, bonding in humiliation. The rest of the show chugged

along just as it should. "9 to 5" was flawless, "Eye of the Tiger" inspiring, "Fame" better than it'd ever been the whole tour—maybe except the time when I'd been in it.

"It's the Hard Knock Life" got tons of laughs and reminded me how much I love to dance—maybe I would try the class that Amy took after all. "Stayin' Alive" sizzled, and the crowd sang along with "The NeverEnding Story."

When "Ghostbusters" began, most of the seven girls from the ranch house in Dallas huddled together backstage. Due to costume changes, this was the only place our new number could go in the show; we'd swapped out "Magic" for it.

"It's almost time," Amy whispered. She looked rad in her black-and-white-striped crop top and black shorts that ballooned out from her waist.

Mrs. Johnson had been thrilled when Amy had let her in on the secret, but there wasn't time for Mrs. Johnson to make us real costumes, so we'd cobbled together outfits from our own duffel bags combined with clothes borrowed from others in the cast—all black and white except a few pieces of neon.

Amy's neon was the hot pink fingerless glove on her left hand. I had the matching one on my right. For the rest of my costume, I wore a black-and-white tiered miniskirt, borrowed from Courtney, and my freshly washed sleeveless polo, which Tuesday had knotted at my hip. My hair was crimped and piled into a high side ponytail, and I had to admit, I felt pretty rad.

"I hope it's cool," I said, shifting in my mismatched high-tops.

One was Amy's, and one belonged to Holly—one black and one white.

"It's definitely cool," Christy said, walking up behind us. She smiled sneakily and undid the top button on her "NeverEnding" costume, revealing neon green underneath. "I layered."

"Smart," I said, my insides doing cartwheels. *Now* I was nervous.

Christy dropped her outer costume like snakeskin. Over her short and sleeveless neon green unitard, she threw on a black off-the-shoulder cropped sweatshirt, then smiled brightly.

Courtney handed her a flashlight. Mine was dangling from my wrist.

"This is going to be fun," Christy said. "I love performing new numbers!" She looked at me earnestly. "And this one's special because it's for you."

"It's not just for me," I corrected her. "It's for anyone who's ever felt rejected."

"That's why this is going to be awesome," Amy said.

"And I'm psyched to perform with you nerds again!" Kris chimed in, peering around the curtain toward the box in the sky. "Mr. Schneider better not forget to leave the lights off in the beginning."

"He won't. I reminded him." Holly jogged up, winded. "I rehearsed with him a ton. I made him a list. His part is super-duper important."

"Oh, dang, 'Ghostbusters' is almost over," Kris said. "Courtney, Amy, let's go!"

Kris took off in her fishnet top toward the back hallway, Courtney and Amy trailing behind. They'd take the stage from the opposite wing.

I inhaled with all my might, then blew out the bad air and the embarrassment and disappointment of liking someone who didn't like me back and the worry about my brother and whether things were changing with me and Wes, not to mention that the school year was rolling in like a freight train.

I pulled back my shoulders and lifted my chin, deciding to be in the moment. Not back where I was when the tour started, when I couldn't see who Joey was. Not who I'd be at school—hopefully a girl who could talk to people without tripping over her words. Definitely a girl with a healthy brother—one cleared to play football under close supervision. Maybe a girl who someone could like back sometime.

I wasn't past Stevie or future Stevie—I was *now* Stevie.

Channeling Christy, I tightened my ponytail.

I was invincible.

IN THE VIDEO we'd all watched together on MTV in Dallas, Pat Benatar slowly saunters into the scene with a bunch of people lighting her path with flashlights. In our version of "Invincible," we slowly walked in from the wings, flashlight beams doing figure eights on the floor perfectly in sync with one another and

the music as we made our way into a staggered line: Amy, me, then Tuesday in the front and Holly, Courtney, Christy, and Kris in the back.

At the twenty-second mark, we turned off and set down our lights, and just like he was supposed to, Mr. Schneider aimed the spotlight at Amy. Given her love of all things horror, it was fitting that she was the one to lip-synch the first line about a mysterious, bloody road.

The spotlight fell on me, and right after I did the part about sudden darkness filling the air, Mr. Schneider made the audience gasp by turning out the lights completely. I giggled with happiness right before he cranked them all on for the duration of the song.

The rest of us danced backup while Holly and Kris lip-synched the next few lyrics, and then right before the chorus, all of us stepped together into a tight huddle, Tuesday and Amy on the floor in front; Christy; Kris, and me on our knees; and Holly and Courtney standing behind, moving in such perfect unison, I felt like we were one mega-powerful person.

It's a do-or-die situation
We will be invincible

Like Christy had wanted, we did signs along with the chorus, and every time I did the sign we were using for invincible, UNBEATABLE, my nails dug into my palm, the muscles in my arms tensed, my jaw clenched.

The lyrics got to the part about there being nowhere to run

anymore. I felt like I had been running from things, or at least shying away from meeting new friends or doing new things because I was afraid of failing or being rejected. But then I *was* rejected, by the boy I'd had a crush on for two whole years, and I'd survived it. I was stronger, and had made stronger bonds, because of it.

Performing that song with those girls on that stage after my very first tour and almost an entire month away from home made me feel like my heart was so full it might burst into a billion tiny pieces. It was the first of many, many times we'd perform "Invincible" since Margo would insist on adding it to the show.

Everyone in the cast loved it—audiences loved it. And it never would have happened if I hadn't opened up and tried something new.

The choreo was strong and sharp, like shouting—not meanly, but proudly. My mom looked like she was crying after I did a triple turn that made the audience go wild when Pat Benatar sang, "Yeaaaaaaah!"

At the end, we stood in a straight line, taking up the whole stage, wide stances, chins high, fists clenched in the UNBEATABLE sign as the music faded, unmoving except for our quick breaths and rapid heartbeats. I heard cheers from the wings and glanced over to see Brandon clapping so fiercely I bet his palms stung. He looked so proud of me, it made me tear up.

Next to Brandon, Joey nodded at me, smiling in a way that

told me he was seeing a different Stevie, too. That maybe he'd underestimated me. That maybe I was cooler than he'd thought. That maybe . . .

Eyes back on the audience, I laughed softly to myself. Whatever Joey was realizing, whatever he was thinking right then, whatever he was considering . . .

I laughed again.

Whatever it was, I didn't care.

Acknowledgments

Synchronicity was inspired by a real-life performing group that I was part of from kindergarten to high school. It's not in any way affiliated with a current performing group in Atlanta—though I'd love to see one of their shows someday!

In my performing days, my mom sewed most (or all?) of the costumes; she did everything from satin appliques on sweatshirts to poodle skirts to an intricate parrot getup I wore with pride. Thank you, Mom, for your energy and dedication, and for the millions of miraculous ways you make me, and all of us, feel loved for being exactly who we are.

My favorite tour was of the East Coast, which inspired the destinations in *We Built This City*. My Brandon on that tour was

my sister, Erin, whom I idolized as a kid and live three minutes from as an adult. All the pigs in the universe to you, my dearest sister and friend. And to the rest of my clan, thank you. I am the luckiest human to have such supportive and hilarious people to call family, from my dad, who is not from Portland; to my beautifully insightful husband; to my brothers, brother-in-law, sisters-in-law, nieces and nephews, aunts and uncles, cousins, and co-parent; to my reason for being—my favorites—my daughters. I positively adore all of you.

My lifelong bestie, Brad, was an original member of the group and an early *We Built This City* reader. I frequently, frantically texted him things like: SEND ME A PICTURE OF YOURSELF IN JUNIOR HIGH IMMEDIATELY and WOULD YOU HAVE WORN HALF OF A BFF FRIENDSHIP NECKLACE WHEN WE WERE KIDS, YES OR NO? Brad put it best when he said, "I'm not Wes, you're not Stevie, but their friendship has the spirit of ours." My dear friend, I love you times infinity. I'm on the edge of your stage forever.

The whole reason we had these experiences in the first place was Brad's amazing mom and group founder, Jackie Taylor. Wanting to make performing arts accessible to both hearing and Deaf audiences, Jackie called the group Stagehands. In addition to lip-synching and dancing, we signed along to the music, which kicked off my appreciation for Deaf culture and is why I felt it was important to have representatives from the Deaf community in the book.

Unfortunately, I didn't keep up with signing as an adult, but I'm thrilled that one of my daughters is taking American Sign Language in high school—she's reconnecting me with the beautiful language and culture. And I'm so thankful that her American Sign Language teacher, Paige Friedli, and Angie Bitner Yepsen, one of my former Stagehands castmates, provided feedback specific to the Deaf community.

Stacey Barney, it's hard to put into words how much you mean to me—I might have to make you a mixtape. Until then, I'll just say thank you for all of it, from the smarts to the silliness. I couldn't ask for a better editor and I'm so grateful for your friendship and cat humor. My sincerest thanks also extend to Caitlin Tutterow, Kelley Brady, Cindy De la Cruz, and the entire marketing and sales team at Penguin/Nancy Paulsen Books.

And Dan. Wow. Thank you for having my back for fourteen years and counting. I'm forever proud to call you my agent and friend, filter or no filter. A huge thank-you, too, to Cecilia de la Campa and Torie Doherty-Munro at Writers House, and to editors worldwide who've cheered on *We Built This City*.

Finally, thank you to the librarians, teachers, booksellers, and book lovers everywhere who've supported me. For as long as I can remember, I wanted to be an author. I'm thankful every day to those of you who keep reading.

ALSO BY CAT PATRICK

Paper Heart

Tornado Brain

Just Like Fate, with Suzanne Young

The Originals

Revived

Forgotten

WE BUILT THIS CITY